Praise for Pond

Named a Best Book of 2016 by *Elle*, *New York Magazine*,
the *San Francisco Chronicle*, *The Huffington Post*, BuzzFeed,
Electric Literature, *BookPage*, and *Publishers Weekly*

Shortlisted for the International Dylan Thomas Prize

"A sharp, funny, and eccentric debut . . . [that] makes the case for Bennett as an innovative writer of real talent. . . . *Pond* reminds us that small things have great depths."
—*The New York Times Book Review*

"Dazzling . . . exquisitely written and daring."   —*O, The Oprah Magazine*

"A work of fiction that will make you feel pleasantly insane . . . It is also funny . . . unnerving . . . sensitive to the point of being porous . . . lucid, practical, and excruciatingly cognizant of what is normal."
—*The New Yorker*

"Bennett's prose—ardent, addictively obsessive-compulsive, a little feral—is from another galaxy, or maybe another century. Her delight in nature and gardening can be kookily romantic . . . and yet one could also imagine her taking an improbably cheerful seat among the modernists. . . . A man alone is a visionary; a woman alone is a witch—or worse, Bridget Jones. But Bennett spins something entirely different from her separateness, a kind of philosophy of being in the world as a writer both refreshing and hard-won."
—*Vogue*

"Innovative, beguiling . . . meditative . . . a fresh new voice from seemingly out of nowhere . . . Reading Bennett's book of loosely linked stories is a lovely retreat from the cacophony of contemporary life."
—*Los Angeles Times*

"Ms. Bennett has a voice that leans over the bar and plucks a button off your shirt. It delivers the sensations of Edna O'Brien's rural Irish world by way of Harold Pinter's clipped dictums. . . . [She] seems to know exactly what to take seriously. She puts us inside a complicated, teeming mind, and she doesn't dabble in forced epiphanies. . . . [Her] sensibility here feels like the tip of a deep iceberg, and I'll be in line to read whatever she publishes next. Her witty misanthropy is here to ward off mental scurvy."

—Dwight Garner, *The New York Times*

"This Woolfian novella will challenge all your ideas of narrative. Dreamlike fragments of a life drift in and out of frame, with startling prose that will make your usual perspective feel like sleepwalking." —*Elle*

"[Bennett's] is a mind in attentive communion with itself, building baroque and beautiful cloud castles of thought to distract from the storms of the real." —*The Wall Street Journal*

"What Bennett aims at is nothing short of a re-enchantment of the world. . . . This is a truly stunning debut, beautifully written and profoundly witty." —*The Guardian*

"[A] cool, curious dive into a world of minutiae . . . intense, and often wickedly funny." —*The Christian Science Monitor*

"Elegant and intoxicating . . . Boldly defying convention, *Pond* is an exceptional debut with beautiful hidden depths." —Minneapolis *Star Tribune*

"A fascinating and utterly immersive reading experience that speaks volumes about the author's creative process and delivers insights in droves . . . Compulsively readable." —*San Francisco Chronicle*

"Exhilarating . . . Put[s] Knausgaard to shame. This is a woman at her most comfortable, her most confident. . . . I think someone should award [Bennett] a great prize so that she can write us all something new." —*The Cut*

"*Pond* express[es] [Bennett's] unique sensibility in deceptively simply, delightfully unsettled prose. . . . We'll be hearing more from this formidably gifted young writer." —*The Boston Globe*

"The sort of avant-garde opus destined to put its author on the map alongside modern-day prose stylists of the highest order . . . This collection is for wiseasses and weirdos, a cathedral of strange sentences . . . built upon the singular experience of being a human being. . . . [A] gorgeous book."

—*Los Angeles Review of Books*

"Muddiness is not typically a positive description for a narrative, but this mud is sparkling, full of mica and minerals that glitter with color when the sun's rays hit. It's through this glistening mud that Bennett's readers get to mudlark, mucking about in prose that is alternatively deliberate and crisp, surrealistic and unknowable, to find real gems of observation and language. . . . Deeply satisfying and refreshing . . . Bennett stomps all over writing-dude-in-nature territory without having to set a foot off her main character's property line." —*The New Republic*

"Sharp and witty . . . wonderfully discursive . . . Bennett . . . writes through the dramatic into something deeper, and the result is a reverie of 'fervid primary visions,' the dredging of a riverine mind." —*The Millions*

"A phenomenal combination of hilarity and stillness with a weird undercurrent of menace that never quite rises to the surface but always leaves you slightly uneasy even as you are smiling about something brilliant the writer has managed to capture in the short space of a few pages." —*The Awl*

"Impressive indeed." —*Vol. 1 Brooklyn*

"Compelling [and] innovative . . . Bennett's unique portrait of a persona emerges with an intensity and vision not often seen, or felt, in a debut." —*Poets & Writers*

"*Pond*, in its quirky structure and language, calls to mind the Irish fathers of literary modernism Joyce and Beckett. But then it also echoes Woolf's *Mrs. Dalloway*, Carroll's *Alice*, Thoreau's *Walden* and, more contemporarily, Strout's *Olive Kitteridge*. . . . Bennett's narrator is a funny, self-deprecating, observant, opinionated, earthy woman whose mind grasps every detailed string of her rural life and gives it a pull to reveal her curiosity and contented solitude. . . . What a treasure, this woman!" —*Shelf Awareness*

"A formally inventive work that slips past traditional storytelling to focus on impression as it chronicles the interior life of a single, unnamed woman dwelling on Ireland's coast." —*Library Journal*

"Innovative and elegant . . . In her celebration of minutiae, Bennett recreates the experience of a believable, uniquely captivating persona. *Pond* deserves to be discovered and dived into, so thoroughly does Bennett submerge readers into her meticulously dazzling world."

—*Booklist* (starred review)

"Captivating . . . Bennett has achieved something strange, unique, and undeniably wonderful." —*Publishers Weekly* (starred review)

"A touch of William Gaddis. A touch of Lydia Davis. A touch of Samuel Beckett. A touch of Edna O'Brien. And yet Claire-Louise Bennett's *Pond* feels entirely unique. Quiet and luxurious all at once, this will be one of the most sensational debuts of the year."

—Colum McCann, author of *Let the Great World Spin*

"Claire-Louise Bennett sets the conventions of literary fiction ablaze in this ferociously intelligent and funny debut. Don't be fooled by *Pond*'s small size. It contains multitudes." —Jenny Offill, author of *Dept. of Speculation*

"*Pond* is brilliant—sharp and absorbing, compassionate and funny—and Claire-Louise Bennett is a deeply original writer with talent to spare. I can't stop thinking about this book."

—Molly Antopol, author of *The UnAmericans*

"As brilliant a debut and as distinct a voice as we've heard in years—this is a real writer with the real goods."

—Kevin Barry, author of *Beatlebone* and *City of Bohane*

"I'd heard more good whispers about *Pond* than almost any other debut this year. . . . These stories are intelligent and funny, innovative and provocative, and it's impossible to read them without thinking that here is a writer who has only just begun to show what she can do."

—Eimear McBride, author of *A Girl Is a Half-Formed Thing*

"Wielding a wry but implacable logic, Claire-Louise Bennett dives under the surface of 'ordinary' experiences and things to reveal their supreme and giddy illogic. Like . . . Lydia Davis . . . she writes an impeccable affectless prose that almost magically arrives at something extraordinary."

—Chris Kraus, author of *I Love Dick*

POND

Claire-Louise Bennett

RIVERHEAD BOOKS

New York

RIVERHEAD BOOKS
An imprint of Penguin Random House LLC
375 Hudson Street
New York, New York 10014

Earlier versions of some of these stories appeared in *The Penny Dreadful*,
The White Review, *3:AM Magazine*, and *The Stinging Fly*.
Jacket art: detail of *Fair is foul and foul is fair*,
© 2015 by Margriet Smulders (margrietsmulders.nl)

The Library of Congress has catalogued the Riverhead hardcover edition as follows:

Names: Bennett, Claire-Louise, author.
Title: Pond / Claire-Louise Bennett.
Description: First American edition. | New York : Riverhead Books, 2016.
Identifiers: LCCN 2016002762 | ISBN 9780399575891 (hardcover)
Subjects: BISAC: FICTION / Literary. Contemporary Women. Psychological.
Classification: LCC PR6102.E562 A6 2016 | DDC 823/.92—dc23
LC record available at http://lccn.loc.gov/2016002762
p.   cm.

First Riverhead hardcover edition: July 2016
First Riverhead trade paperback edition: July 2017
Riverhead trade paperback ISBN: 9780399575907

Printed in the United States of America
3   5   7   9   10   8   6   4

Book design by Marysarah Quinn

CONTENTS

For now in every exuberant joy there is heard an undertone of terror, or else a wistful lament over an irrecoverable loss. It is as though . . . nature were bemoaning the fact of her fragmentation, her decomposition into separate individuals.

FRIEDRICH NIETZSCHE, *The Birth of Tragedy*

Could it be that any apartment, any one at all, might eventually become a burrow? Would any place eventually welcome me into its dim, warm, reassuring, kindly light?

NATALIA GINZBURG, "A Place to Live"

Wolves in shells are crueller than stray ones.

GASTON BACHELARD, *The Poetics of Space*

POND

Voyage in the Dark

FIRST OF ALL, it seemed to us that you were very handsome. And the principal windows of your house were perfectly positioned to display a blazing reflection at sunset. One evening while walking back from the fields this effect was so dramatic we thought your rooms were burning. We liked nothing better than to rake the tinkling gravel on your drive, then to climb an impeccable tree along its passage and wait. We would hear the engine loud in the valley, followed by a thrilling silence within which we would wave our boots and imagine the leather grip of your hands upon the steering wheel, left and right. Oh, but we were only little girls, little girls, there on the cusp of female individuation, not little girls for long. The other two hung back by the brook with cups on sticks while I made my way over the wall into your ornamental garden, lay down upon the unfeasible grass and fell to sleep wrapped about a lilac seashell, which was of course my most cherished possession.

Morning, Noon & Night

SOMETIMES A BANANA with coffee is nice. It ought not to be too ripe—in fact there should be a definite remainder of green along the stalk, and if there isn't, forget about it. Though admittedly that is easier said than done. Apples can be forgotten about, but not bananas, not really. They don't in fact take at all well to being forgotten about. They wizen and stink of putrid and go almost black.

Oatcakes along with it can be nice, the rough sort. The rough sort of oatcake goes especially well with a banana by the way—by the way, the banana might be chilled slightly. This can occur in the fridge overnight of course, depending on how prescient and steadfast one is about one's morning victuals, or, it might be, and this in fact is much more preferable, there's a nice cool windowsill where a bowl especially for fruit can always be placed.

A splendid deep wide sill with no wooden overlay, just the plastered stone, nice and chilly: the perfect place for a bowl. Even a few actually, a few bowls in fact. The sill's that big it can accommodate three sizeable bowls very well without appearing the least bit encumbered. It's quite pleasant, then, to unpack the pannier bags and arrange everything intently in the bowls upon the sill. Aubergine, squash, asparagus and small vine tomatoes look terribly swish together and it's no surprise at all that anyone would experience a sudden urge at any time during the day to sit down at once and attempt with a palette and brush to convey the exotic patina of such an irrepressible gathering of illustrious vegetables, there on the nice cool windowsill.

Pears don't mix well. Pears should always be small and organised nose to tail in a bowl of their very own and perhaps very occasionally introduced to a stem of the freshest red currants, which ought not to be hoisted like a mantle across the freckled belly of the topmost pear, but strewn a little further down so that some of the scarlet berries loll and bask between the slowly shifting gaps.

Bananas and oatcakes are by the way a very satisfactory substitute for those mornings when the time for porridge has quite suddenly passed. If a neighbour has been overheard or the towels folded the day's too far in and porridge, at this point, will feel vertical and oppressive, like a gloomy repast from the underworld. As such, in all likelihood, a submerged stump of resentment will begin to perk up right at the first mouthful and will very likely preside dumbly over the entire day. Until, finally, at around four o'clock, it becomes unfairly but inevitably linked to someone close by, to a particular facet of their behaviour in fact, a perpetually irksome facet that can be readily isolated and enlarged and thereupon pinpointed as the prime cause of this most foreboding sense of resentment, which has been on the rise, inexplicably, all day, since that first mouthful of porridge.

Some sort of black jam in the middle of porridge is very nice, very striking in fact. And then a few flaked almonds. Be careful though, be very careful with flaked almonds; they are not at all suitable for morose or faint-hearted types and shouldn't be flung about like confetti because almonds are not in the least like confetti. On the contrary, flaked almonds ought not to touch one another and should be organised in simple patterns, as on the side of a pavlova, and then they are quite pretty and perfectly innocuous. But shake out a palmful of flaked almonds and you'll see they closely resemble fingernails that have come away from a hand which has just seen the light of day.

Black jam and blanched fingernails, slowly sinking into

the oozing burgoo! Lately, in the mornings, Ravel, played several times over, has been a very nice accompaniment indeed. And this, for now, is how, with minor variations, the day begins.

My own nails are doing very well as a matter of fact, indeed, I'm not sure they have ever done better. If you must know I painted them in the kitchen last Wednesday after lunch, and the shade I painted them right there in the kitchen is called Highland Mist. Which is a very good name, a very apt name, as it turns out. Because, you see, the natural colour of my nail, both the white part and the pink part, is still just about visible beneath the polish, it hasn't been completely obscured. And as time passes the polish doesn't chip away as such, it just sort of thins out around the edges, so now, as well as being able to see the white part and the pink part, the soot beneath the tips is also clearly visible. There, through the mist, which is of course the colour of heather, I can see coal dust beneath my fingernails. When the nails aren't painted at all this dirt has no other effect besides looking grubby and unkempt, but under the thinning sheen of Highland Mist something further occurs to me when I consider my hands. They look like the hands of someone very charming and refined who has had to dig themselves up out of some dank and wretched spot they really shouldn't have fallen into. And that amuses me, that really amuses me.

Indeed, it wouldn't be entirely unwarranted to suggest that I might, overall, have the appearance and occasionally emanate the demeanour of someone who grows things. That's to say, I might, from time to time, be considered earthy in its most narrow application. However, truth is, I have propagated very little and possess only a polite curiosity for horticultural endeavours. It's quite true that bright green parsley grows out of a pot near my door but I did not grow it from seed, not at all—I simply bought it already sprouted from a nearby supermarket, turned the plant out its plastic carton and shoved its compacted network of roots and soil here, into the pot next to my door.

Prior to that, some years ago, when I lived near the canal, I could plainly see from my bedroom window a most idyllic piece of land, encircled by the gardens of houses in back-to-back streets which thereby rendered it landlocked and enticing. It seemed impossible to get to the garden yet when I tore after a cat early one day he led me directly to it, whereupon he skedaddled sharpish and left me a tortured wren to cradle and fold. The wren had sung above my head for many weeks in the sunshine while I wrote letters in the morning and so it was only natural for me to cry out when I found it maimed and silent on the moss beneath the privet hedge. I was so upset I wanted to take that cat to a hot pan and sear its foul backside in an explosion of oil. I'll make you hiss you little shit. Never mind. I was in the garden that nobody owned or imposed upon and now that I had come here once I could come here again, surely. That's how it worked when I was a child anyhow, and I don't suppose these matters change a great deal.

I made sly enquiries just as a child does but unfortunately in contrast to a child I was listened to rather too attentively and so I quickly devised a wholesome reason for wishing to know who owned the land and whether I might visit it from time to time. It would be a very excellent place to grow things I'm sure I said and despite having never demonstrated any enthusiasm for gardening before and despite my statement of interest being really rather vague my proposition was taken seriously and since it turned out the land was in fact owned by the Catholic Church I was directed to the large house on the corner where the parish priest himself resided. This development was not something I had foreseen, truth be told I'd had no purposeful intentions. I think I just fancied the idea of having a secluded place to stand about in now and then, a secret garden if you like. And I should never have said a word about it because as usual the minute I did it all became quite misshapen and not what I had in mind at all, and yet there was something so alien and absurd about how it was all progressing that I couldn't help but go right along with it.

He was pleasantly perfunctory and did not mention anything at all about God, though he did enunciate the word bounty rather pointedly, but I didn't flinch. Where do you live, he said. Over in that house there, I said, and pointed through the window at a house across the road. He didn't look in the direction of my finger, it was quite sufficient for him that I could stand where I was and at the same time point to my house, and so it was settled. I do not remember the interior of the priest's house. I think the wallpaper in the hallway might have been sage green. It could be the case that I went in no further than the hallway. Perhaps I just stood at the door on the street looking in at the hallway. And then down at the plastic step. Yes, I believe he was wearing trainers in fact.

Clearing a decent area of ground and making it ready for planting potatoes was hard and monotonous work added to which early spring tends to be rather humid here and indeed it was so that particular year. I do not know fully what drove me to deracinate thick and fuzzy weeds like that every day in the premature heat. I often stopped and stood quite still, wondering what hopes my mind had just then been taken up with, but I could seldom recall. However, in spite of my own bemusement, for the first time in my adult life other people knew exactly what I was doing. It was as plain as day to them. I'd come back with the tools and lean them against the house wall and go inside to wash my hands and it would be quite clear to anyone who saw me what I had been doing that day. I believe during that period people were, notwithstanding two or three specific incidents, conspicuously more agreeable towards me.

As with most mensurable areas of life I demonstrated no ambition whatsoever as a grower and selected to cultivate low-maintenance crops only. Potatoes, spinach and broad beans. That was it. That was enough. People told me what a cinch it was to grow courgettes, squash, marrow, carrots, but nothing had changed really—I hadn't suddenly become a gardener, and I resented being spoken to as though I had. The plants were coming on quite nicely when I received an invitation to speak at a very eminent university across the water upon a subject I was very interested in indeed— though not necessarily in a meritorious way. That's to say my interest was far too personal and not strictly academic and so my methodology came across as nostalgic and my perspective rather naive since I ignored the usual critical frameworks which were anyhow quite incomprehensible to me and instead pilfered haphazardly from the entire history of Western literature in order to strengthen my argument, which I cannot now recall. It had something to do with love. About the essential brutality of love. About those adventitious souls who deliberately seek out love as a prime agent of total self-immolation. Yes, that's right. It attempted to show that in the whole history of literature love is quite routinely depicted as an engulfing process of ecstatic suffering which finally, mercifully, obliterates us and delivers us to oblivion. Dismembered and packed off. Something like that. Something along those lines. I am mad about you. I am going out of my mind. My soul burns for you. I am inflamed. There is nothing now, nothing except you. Gone, quite gone. That kind of thing. I don't think it went down very well.

In fact I think it was considered rather unsophisticated and I remember feeling, despite my new floral chemise, suddenly sullen and practically gothic. Actually, now that I come to think of it, I think the gist of my argument was simply that love is indeed a vicious and divine disintegration of selfhood and that artistic representations of it as such aren't at all uncommon or outlandish and have nothing whatsoever to do with endeavouring to shock an audience. There was an awful lot of violence you see in the work of the playwright the conference was reputedly reassessing and by and large that violence had hitherto been widely interpreted as nothing more than a dramatic strategy designed to shock, which I could never quite accept because how on earth is there anything shocking about violence? Anyway, I must confess, in order to establish a perennial language of love that testified to the abominable emancipation that is brought on by want of another I did in fact reference not only Sappho, Seneca, Novalis, Roland Barthes, Denis de Rougement and Dutch historian Johan Huizinga, I also included lyrics by PJ Harvey and Nick Cave, with the somewhat misplaced intention of demonstrating that it just never stops. That the desire to come apart irrevocably will always be as strong as, if not stronger than, the drive to establish oneself. *As deep as ink and black, black as the deepest sea.*

Afterwards, when people were milling about and nodding in little groups, and I wasn't sure which of the several exits to make immediate use of, one of the academic big guns approached me and commented upon my paper. This all happened several years ago by the way—and I'm not absolutely sure why I'm recounting it here since it hardly situates me in a very flattering light—anyway, I don't recall exactly what he said to me, but it was exceedingly condescending and I very very clearly remember thinking why don't you fall over. Why don't you become tangled in some cables near the screen at the front on your way out and fall over and why don't you smack your head off a very sharp corner of the desk where earlier I sat and delivered my oh so charming missive and cut your head open ever so slightly so that a little bit of blood drops out. Just a little trickle of blood so that you don't look injured, only stupid and a bit iffy. Thank you very much, I said. And suddenly my back went cold so I deduced that the outside must after all be right there behind me; I turned around and walked towards it and very soon the ground did in fact change. It was wet and the car park was almost empty and smelt exclusively of dishcloths.

I may as well mention that I was staying with a girl I'd met in London the previous year. She was a very gifted academic and her ability to formulate a rousing opinion in response to something that had just happened or had just been said never ceased to impress and baffle me. How anyone could sally forth thoughts that were unfailingly well-formed and de rigueur, so soon and in any situation, was quite beyond me. She lived in a terrace house with several other postgraduate students, one of whom was a bloke as a matter of fact, and later, when my friend had gone to bed, he came into the sitting room where I sat with a large book flopped in my lap and put a hot water bottle underneath my toes. We didn't kiss then; we kissed later, a few weeks later. I flew home first and then we wrote to each other and then we really needed to see each other. So I went back, and then we kissed.

None of that has anything to do with now by the way. Despite how promising I seem to have made the encounter with the man and the hot water bottle sound it was in fact an ill-starred liaison and, perhaps less surprisingly, the inviability of my academic career eventually acquired a palpability of such insidious force that one day I came out of a shop unwrapping a pack of cigarettes and went nowhere for approximately half an hour. My wherewithal had quite dried up you see, I'd snubbed it for so long it had completely dried up and so I had come to a standstill, not knowing at all whether to turn left or go right. And the chief reason why I moved after approximately half an hour is because people continually approached me to enquire if the bus had already come and gone. I don't know, I said. I don't know, I said again. I don't know. And then it was as though they backed away and vanished completely and I was left standing absolutely and purposelessly alone—I don't think I've experienced a sense of fundamental redundancy to that extent since. The hopelessness of everything I was trying to occupy myself with was at last glaringly crystal clear.

But the potato plants were still growing! I went over to see my upbeat boyfriend many times and the potatoes and spinach and broad beans didn't mind one bit and sometimes while I was away I would lie in bed next to him unable to sleep and would think of the potatoes and spinach and broad beans out there in the dark and I'd splay my fingers towards the ceiling and feel such yearning! I could recall the soil very well, how dark it was and the smell of it—as if it had never before been opened up, and the canal was nearby, and the moon was always overhead, and spiders would get off their webs for a bit and tentatively come into contact with the still edges of things. We didn't get along very well but this had no bearing whatsoever on our sexual rapport which was impervious and persuasive and made every other dwindling aspect of our relationship quite irrelevant for some time. We wrote each other hundreds of lustful emails, and by that I mean graphic and obscene. It was wonderful. I'd never done that before, I'd never written anything salacious before, it was completely new to me and I must say I got the hang of it really very quickly. I wish I'd kept them, I wish I hadn't become quite so unhinged when finally we acknowledged that eighteen months was pretty well as much as we could expect from a relationship based almost entirely upon avid fornication, and thereupon rashly expunged our complete correspondence, which, by then, amounted to almost two thousand emails. I won't be able to write emails like that again you see—that's to say I won't be able to write emails like that for the first time again. And that really was what made them so exciting—using language in a way I'd not used it before, to transcribe such an intimate area of my being that I'd never before attempted to linguistically lay bare. It was very nice I must say to every now and then take a break from cobbling together yet another overwrought academic abstract on more or less the same theme in order to set down, so precisely, how and where I'd like my brains to be fucked right out.

It wasn't all one way of course. He came to see me, and in fact he ate some of the vegetables I'd grown and he said they were lovely, which they were. We ate oranges too, quite often—in fact eating Spanish oranges became a bit of a thing. They are very nice to eat, oranges, when you've been having sex for ages. They cut through the fug and smell very organised, and so a sort of structure resumes and then it is perfectly possible to make a plan, such as going out somewhere nice for dinner.

Still, as I've said, none of this has anything to do with now whatsoever. I don't know what it has to do with and as a matter of fact I'm not sure what now is about either. I can say that I'm waiting for the delivery of two Japanese tapestries I bought in France earlier this year, but even that is off the mark and could very well proffer a misleading impression of me, a rather grand impression perhaps, as if I were supremely but subtly well-off and presided over quite the sequestered emporium of exotic whatnots and recherché objets d'art. Castles in the clouds I'm afraid, truth is, they can hardly be thought of as tapestries at all—they aren't much more than two pieces of old black cloth in two separate frames with some rose-gold flecks here and there, amounting, in one, to a pair of hands, and to a rather forlorn profile in the other. From what I remember of them it seems there had originally been many more stitches and thus a more complete and detailed image but for a reason I cannot at all decipher most of the stitches have been removed. Yet the trace of where they once were is discernible with some effort, as of course are the very small holes, where silken thread, presumably, moved deftly in and out of the cloth. I should think that in here especially they will only ever look like two framed fragments of black cloth. That's if they ever arrive of course—the man bringing them over was due at seven o'clock and it is now gone half past.

After that I lived in a shared house with my very own bathroom. Not an en suite by the way. I don't see what all the fuss is about where en suites are concerned. In my opinion they're nearly always rather dreary, and as a rule I think it's much nicer to leave a room entirely before entering another. Added to which I couldn't stand being naked in my bedroom, even the thought of being naked in sight of my bedroom was quite awful, yet at the same time I couldn't stand being dressed either—dressing myself made me cringe, it felt pathetic and irrelevant, and of course I never stopped knowing that the fingers pushing the buttons up through the holes would be the same fingers that would later push them back out again. Increasingly, very long baths down the hall became my only respite—I'm really not sure what would have happened at all had the two rooms been adjoined. In the end I spent too long in there. Hours and hours in fact. I didn't know where else to go you see. I'd sit at my desk from time to time, but that was all over with. That's right, I'd thrown in the towel at last. It hadn't worked out. I stopped doing what I wasn't really doing and got a job in a bicycle repair shop which turned out to be quite fortuitous because very soon after I began working there I urgently needed a new bike. I had a bike but I needed a new one, a different one, one with gears, one that could go up hills, one that could go up hills and carry shopping, one that felt sturdy and safe at night along roads where there is no light, one that could go up hills.

I SAW IT FIRST through the hedgerow. It was summer and the hedgerow was very thick and actually almost impossible to see through but if you parted the leaves carefully, just a little bit, you could see all the way through—but you had to be careful, because of the bright flowers that extended, like dancers on tiptoes, everywhere among the hedgerow's branches. That can't be it, I said to my friend. Do you think that's it? I stepped back and stood in the road and looked downhill then uphill. It must be it, I said. There's nothing else. It's perfect, she said. I can't believe it, I said. Then we both peered through the hedge silently and I knew that of course this was it.

Place mats aren't really my thing to be perfectly honest but it looks as if I'm going to have to buy some to put beneath the bowls on the windowsill. Evidently the stone there has become rather too cold and possibly a bit damp because the other day an orange went off very quickly and I see today that the aubergine has developed some moist fluff in the shape and hue of an oyster. I ought to go down to the compost bin; it seems I have been putting it off. I think I've lost interest in it actually, it's got very boring. Someone told me the other day that they had worms escaping from theirs, which I thought sounded quite momentous. I like worms and have no problem picking them up, which is unusual and thus gives me a clear advantage in certain situations because it means I can fling them at people if I feel like it and that never fails to cheer me up. There's a blue plastic bowl in the kitchen on the worktop where I collect scraps and skins and teabags and rinds and stalks and weeping leaves and shells etc. for the compost bin and the idea was to use a small-ish bowl so that I would empty it often, daily in fact, but I don't do that. I don't do that and it piles up, it all piles up and sometimes, though this happens rarely, I tip it all into a bigger bowl and just carry on.

Carry on with what? Well, for your information, there are always things that must be done—this, for one thing, after the fire has been lit of course. The birds need feeding at least once a day this time of year. And after a while I make the bed. I go up the steps and take a look in the postbox. I like a coffee first thing. Sometimes I have a banana along with it. Sometimes that's all I need. And the blue bowl gets emptied, or not, into the compost bin. And the enamel bucket taken without fail to the side of the cottage and filled up with coal again and again. And because there is no step everything gets in here so there is never a time when the floor couldn't do with a good sweep. And of course there is always something to fold.

I texted the man, whose estranged wife is a very dear friend of mine, and asked him if he'd fallen asleep—I really couldn't think what else might have happened to him. He texted back right away to say he was en route. He brought a bag of wood with him that had come from trees in his own garden and a bottle of wine that came from the country where his estranged wife—my dear friend—now lives. It was a wine I was familiar with and it was jarring, sort of, to drink it here, at this time, without her. The Japanese frames and their pared back interiors were in a large cotton bag which he leant against the ottoman beneath the mirror. I did not go near the bag and perhaps he supposed I had no real interest in the contents but I didn't want to look at the pieces in front of him, I wanted to be alone, because in that way I wouldn't have to come up with something to say about them. In circumstances when an impression is extended for the benefit of the person looming nearby, whatever is said is rarely anything at all evocative, and the moment it is said something intrinsic is circumvented and cannot be recaptured later on. Anyhow, I didn't mind waiting—waiting was a pleasure in fact. Anticipation, when it occurs, often makes me animated and expansive, as if I am perhaps reviving and honing my senses in preparation for the awaited object: yes indeed, the world is a scintillant and fascinating place when a half-remembered mystery leans within reach. He stayed for an hour and we talked about the three sons and renting apartments abroad and the recent success of a mutual friend and now and then he expressed deliberately autocratic views in order to rile me but in fact he was wasting his time because I could not be offended—on the contrary, I found a great deal to be amused by, and it might be that my irreverent attitude threw him; some people would much rather make you cross it seems. We may have mentioned Christmas, I do not recall. Even after he left I did not go to the bag directly—I took his emptied glass and the wine cooler out to the kitchen, I arranged the wood he'd kindly given me, I hung up a coat—the wine you see had gone gallivanting through my blood and I didn't want to come at the pictures with a giddy head full of fanciful expectation. So I waited awhile longer, until a more subdued atmosphere was restored, and then I went to the bag and lifted out the heavy frames; focused and unfazed—like a connoisseur.

There are six and a half small flowers. Their petals are small and heart-shaped. Scattered about them are individual petals, these are not heart-shaped and they are slightly darker, as if falling further away. A pair of hands reaches up to the flowers, just the outline of a pair of hands and the edge of one sleeve of a kimono. There is a face, turned, not looking up towards the hands, not at all concerned with the hands' activity: the forehead, the heavy eyelids, the pursed lips, and an earring. All of this occurs in just one small diagonal area of the cloth, the rest is in blackness. And it is the same face in the second frame, where there are even fewer stitches. And while I look at this downcast profile and the few vertical lines which denote, again, the fabric of a heavy kimono, I realize I was quite wrong. Nothing had been undone; there hasn't ever been more than this. What I saw, what I can still see when I stand close enough, was the idea—the plan—of course! Whoever created these did not remove stitches with the intention, as I had initially suspected, of beginning again; they'd simply stopped what they were doing. They did not feel obliged to complete the plan and so they did not complete the plan. Just this, just these few details showed enough. And they must have really felt that and been quite satisfied with it, because why else would they have put these two dark fragments into such beautiful frames?

I've put them on the mantelpiece—you could say they've been given pride of place. They are close to one another but not exactly side by side: they are related, but they aren't a pair. Some people don't notice them at all and other people are instantly intrigued by them, in which case I go into the kitchen so they have every opportunity to become utterly absorbed without feeling obliged to talk about it, which would spoil everything. Yes, I could stand in the kitchen maybe and keep an eye on things from there and perhaps one day my heart by then will be right up in the roof of my mouth as I feel someone becoming more and more taken in until finally they call out to me, excited and amazed, and say, "Look at that—she's been holding a parasol all along!"

There were so many flowers already in bloom when I moved in: wisteria, fuchsia, roses, golden chain, and many other kinds of flowering trees and shrubs I do not know the names of—many of them wild—and all in great abundance. The sun shone most days so naturally I spent most days out the front there, padding in and out all day long, and the air was absolutely buzzing with so many different species of bee and wasp, butterfly, dragonfly, and birds, so many birds, and all of them so busy. Everything: every plant, every flower, every bird, every insect, just getting on with it. In the mornings I flitted about my cottage, taking crockery out of the plate rack and organising it into jaunty stacks along the window ledge, slicing peaches and chopping hazelnuts, folding back the quilt and smoothing down the sheet, watering plants, cleaning mirrors, sweeping floors, polishing glasses, folding clothes, wiping casements, slicing tomatoes, chopping spring onions. And then, after lunch, I'd take a blanket up to the top garden and I'd lie down under the trees in the top garden and listen to things.

I would listen to a small beetle skirting the hairline across my forehead. I would listen to a spider coming through the grass towards the blanket. I'd listen to a squabbling pair of blue tits seesawing behind me. I'd listen to the wood-pigeon's wings whack through the middle branches of an ivy-clad beech tree and the starlings on the wires overhead, and the seagulls and swifts much higher still. And each sound was a rung that took me further upwards, and in this way it was possible for me to get up really high, to climb up past the clouds, towards a bird-like exuberance, where there is nothing at all but continuous light and acres of blue. Later on, towards evening, as it got cooler, I would snuggle into myself a little more and listen less and less so that, very slowly, I returned to dusk and earth. And then I'd soon begin to feel very hungry indeed so I'd sling the blanket across one shoulder and head back up to the cottage to start dinner. Which would frequently involve broad beans, lemons, perhaps some spinach, and plenty of chopped walnuts and white cheese.

Chopping.
Morning, noon and night, it seems.
How I love to chop.

WITHIN THESE DEEP STONE WALLS the sound of a large knife pounding against the chopping board is often mellow and euphonious; like a lulling chant it charms and placates me. Other times, late evening especially, the blade's keen reverberation is more rugged and insistent and I have to make a concerted effort to keep my eyes down and my hands steady. I go on with my guillotining and methodically pare down this robust gathering of swanky solanums until they lose colour. Chopping, taking it all to pieces, in a kind of contracted stupor, morning, noon and night; trying not to pay any heed to my reflection in the mirror as I do so. I can't stand that—above all I can't stand to see the reflection of my waist, winding back and forth, there in the mirror just to my right—looking as if it might take flight when I know very well it can't.

First Thing

THE RATCATCHER WOKE ME, I knew he was coming, but I'd had three overflowing beers the night
before and I'd slept through the rat and I wanted to go on
sleeping.

Go on sleeping through the rising birds and through
the horses walking up the hill and through the four cows
rearranging themselves and through the dog that follows
the horses on their way down the hill and through the cat
here and there and through the fox stopping and starting
on the driveway and through the donkey standing, but
the ratcatcher woke me and down the stairs I came

and made us both coffees right away. And because I
wasn't really here I didn't yet know how I like things, so I
put two sugars and milk into my coffee, because that's how
the ratcatcher takes his.

The Big Day

I SAT LATE ONE AFTERNOON for a reason that reso-
lutely refuses to come to mind in my neighbours' house
with my coat on all alone in the room between the kitchen
and the parlour. I don't know where she was, the one who
had answered the door, off in the garden somewhere posi-
tioning a sign I should think because by that time they really
were getting ready for the big day. I had, by then, already
given them bunting so that was not the reason for my being
in my neighbours' house. It's true that besides the bunting I
also gave them a box of coloured straws that someone had
in fact given me one spring around the time of my birthday
perhaps—however I remember distinctly leaving the box
of straws on the wall near the gate to the neighbours' house
on a beautiful afternoon when I was feeling particularly
magnanimous and lithe—hence the capacity to overcome

my growing apprehension and contribute something from under the sink towards the big day. Actually this turned out to be a slightly more bothersome enterprise than I had predicted due to the fact that the box of straws would not stay upright upon the wall. They didn't look too good lying horizontally, which is understandable when you consider that a level straw is a useless straw, so I was stuck at the wall for quite a while, fumbling like a laggard, trying to find a way of propping the box up so that its final position didn't discredit the earnestness of my gesture nor the snazzy appeal of the item it was attempting to convey. There were pink straws and blue ones and yellow ones and perhaps some green ones too. The pink straws were the nicest really because they were very bright and looked surprisingly sophisticated whereas the other colours were not quite so striking and so those straws looked like exhausted flumes that small children come shooting out of in water parks, in landlocked European countries especially. I remember the lido in Bavaria very well in fact and the way the children were very focused, tiptoeing around the wooden sun-loungers all day long collecting glass bottles to return to the dusky hatch beneath the evergreens in exchange for a few pfennigs each time, because it was in fact pfennigs then. That was also an uncannily serene day and I was alone then too, so although

I swam I did not feel brave enough to go all the way to the other side for the reason that when I am alone it is practically impossible for me to gauge distance.

Not only did I still have my coat on but my rucksack was still on my shoulders too and I think I'm right in saying that it felt very consoling and perhaps I wriggled back into its padded girth. The seat I was sitting on was a kitchen chair in the old style and by that time I was quite fagged out since in all likelihood I had just come back from doing circuitous errands in town the like of which often causes my neck and shoulders to turn on me. It could be that there was something from the postbox to give her. That often happens; none of them seem to check the postbox as often as I do which is rather unusual when one takes into account they all seem to receive quite interesting things fairly regularly. Sometimes I take them, these small handcrafted boxes and crammed envelopes, and put them on top of the storage heater where they might well remain for up to a week before I manage to pass them on to the intended recipient. The postbox gets damp you see, causing letters and so on to pucker and leak, so occasionally I am quite diligent about emptying it and other times my mind is such that I just don't care enough about what happens to other people's post. Of course already there were things inside the house here and there that testified to the imminence of the big day, and the reason I sat down at all was to have a look at some visual material and historical information they'd acquired from the landlady. First of all there was a rudimentary map with names written either in or next to the various plotted rectangles which denoted the different cottages that were, at the time of this particular survey, a hundred or so years ago, inhabited by various humans. It is necessary to specify humans because actually it was not always the case that the buildings provided a bolt-hole for people only—my own cottage, for example, was used to store hay for a while and it is likely that from time to time a pregnant cow took refuge there. Attached to this map was a census form which further elaborated on the two-legged inhabitants and the precise dates of their tenure—this was however, no matter how much I tried, of little interest to me. Names, typical names: names you'd see in any number of places around about, on signs above pharmacies and bars, across plastic packages of bacon, for example. Perhaps as often happens I'd misplaced my keys once again and was unable to get into the laundry room to turn my washing out of the machine into the basket so that it could all be carried to the line and hung there to dry.

What difference does it make anyway why I happened to be in the neighbours' house? I don't know why I keep going on about it or indeed why not remembering is irking me so much. What possible meaning will be advanced if I do finally ascertain what had me go over there? Perhaps it was bunting, perhaps it was straws, or to gain access to the washing machine and my laundered clothes, perhaps I was delivering mail, returning a spoon, asking for jam, enquiring as to the whereabouts of my sleeping bag which was for two months tucked unobtrusively behind the tumble dryer and is now nowhere to be seen, perhaps it was to bitch about the rotten sheepdog who comes down the driveway every morning to dispense a slapdash turd between the shed and the outbuilding, or maybe I was spotted coming down the steps and a conversation about the big day was embarked upon and I said yes of course I'd like to come in and finally see the material the landlady has provided especially.

She must have made me a cup of tea anyhow, before she went off to place a cautionary notice next to the pond—which, by the way, has absolutely no depth whatsoever. If it were left up to me I wouldn't put a sign next to a pond saying pond, either I'd write something else, such as Pig Swill, or I wouldn't bother at all. I know what the purpose of it is, I know it's to prevent children from coming upon the pond too quickly and toppling in, but still I don't quite agree with it. It's not that I want children to fall into the pond per se, though I can't really see what harm it would do them; it's that I can't help but assess the situation from the child's perspective. And quite frankly I would be disgusted to the point of taking immediate vengeance if I was brought to a purportedly magical place one afternoon in late September and thereupon belted down to the pond, all by myself most likely, only to discover the word pond scrawled on a poxy piece of damp plywood right there beside it. Oh I'd be hopping. That sort of moronic busybodying happens with such galling regularity throughout childhood of course and it never ceases to be utterly vexing. One sets off to investigate you see, to develop the facility to really notice things so that, over time, and with enough practice, one becomes attuned to the earth's embedded logos and can experience the enriching joy of moving about in deep and direct accordance with things. Yet invariably this vital process is abruptly thwarted by an idiotic overlay of literal designations and inane alerts so that the whole terrain is obscured and inaccessible until eventually it is all quite formidable. As if the earth were a colossal and elaborate deathtrap. How will I ever make myself at home here if there are always these meddlesome scaremongering signs everywhere I go.

She was in the garden and I stayed on the kitchen chair with my rucksack strapped to my back and my coat still zipped up to my chin and I must have had a cup of tea with me surely otherwise I wouldn't have stayed there very long when in fact I stayed there a good while. I think I liked sitting there actually; I think I felt as if I'd just come home from school on a Thursday. Nobody was taking any notice of me yet there was a lovely comforting sensation that beneficent things were being done for me somewhere. I think, as human experiences go, that is one of my favourite ones.

What they'd done was this: they'd made a sort of collage of images on several different sheets of paper and I suppose the idea was that they'd somehow affix these sheets of paper down below in the garden room which was I believe the intended epicentre of the big day's planned activities. The photographs were all contemporaneous— that's to say they were all taken in the early 90s, 1990s that is, which is when my landlady and her sister obtained the site and commenced the all-out task of redeeming and reviving the various ailing properties and untrained gardens therein. And it is likely that some photographs were taken on one day and some more a few months later and yet more again after a year or two, that kind of thing, because there are changes, remarkable changes, and it is possible, from the photographs, to see what it was and what it became. And what it became, by the way, is not what it is now, and what it is now is not what it was either. She stands there in the mud, my landlady, which needless to say there was an awful lot of, yet it must be mentioned because I'd never seen mud quite like it—feudal and rich, almost igneous in fact, as if suddenly it would rupture and divulge a beast of fire or turn in on itself in a molten whirlpool of dark flashing water. It was quite mesmerising and I wondered what it must have been like, to go over it day after day. I'm sure she must have felt tremendous, really quite tremendous; which doesn't always make things easy of course. She is wearing boots, naturally, and her blond hair looks voluminous and very bright, in contrast to all the unearthed things around her, and behind her is the back wall, marbled with lichen and moss, of the building where I live.

The sensation that someone somewhere was doing something nice for me, such as placing a piece of breaded fish onto a preheated baking tray in a fan-assisted oven, dissipated the instant the sun left the room; the commonplace order of things reasserted itself with an inhumane brusqueness, and since nothing in my immediate locale belonged to me I felt useless and insipid. Although I was quite alone I had nonetheless managed to outstay my welcome. I got up and it may have been getting dark by then and perhaps I met my neighbour on the step on my way out and wished her good night. I would have to find my keys now. I would have to find my keys and open the front door. I would open the front door and march straight in, and into the kitchen I would go whereupon I would unbridle myself of the rucksack stuffed and shuffling with choice provisions and set it down upon the green cold tiles of the worktop and the contents would slump and settle again yet they would ere long be unpacked and divided but first I would ferret out the cheese buffered there between the pouches of ham and two tapered slices of the purest cheese I'd eat forthwith and this would briefly alleviate me of all other pressing duties so I would gaze awhile out the windowpane and I would not deign to get involved in anything, not one single blessed thing out there. No way. Cheese appeased and back on track I would smooth out the receipt of purchase along the green cold tiles of the counter and I would mull over this inventory of fine produce as if it had no fealty whatsoever to the many articles piled up around about me. Very good, I would say. Good job all in all. Thump thump. Praise be. And on it would go with little pieces of restorative cheese in between, until the surfaces and edges and handles and lids all fell to silence at last.

. . .

A FEW DAYS before the big day a Portaloo appeared to the left of the shed as I see it out the kitchen window. There was, needless to say, very soon a sign stuck upon it saying Toilet. I hadn't seen it coming, that's to say I wasn't here when it was delivered—I had been notified of its necessity however so it did not come as much of a surprise to me when I looked out the kitchen window one morning and saw a Portaloo next to the shed. Other more salubrious indications that a big day was on the horizon included a scant but wholesome menu written in alternating colours on a slate board which was propped up for all to see—once they got here of course—next to the kitchen window of the main house. And of course there was a lot of walking to and fro so that I could hear, especially in the bathroom and up in my bed, the sound of gravel underfoot on and on from early in the morning to sometime later in the evening for days on end. Since my attitude towards the big day had been dependably inconsistent I was not prevailed upon to help with the many preparations under way and this was as well for everyone because a lack of enthusiasm for a project makes me very clear-headed indeed and I would in all likelihood have developed a keen sense of how it should all come together and would therefore have taken over completely. In the days before the Portaloo arrived my mind tipped back and forth, quite unable to settle upon a decision about whether or not I'd be around for the big day. All this vacillating came to a rapid standstill once the Portaloo had been installed, as such, whenever I looked across at the Portaloo I regarded it as an ally, an ally in from-the-hip decision making, and I felt nothing but gratitude towards its moulded and unerring bulk. Cool Portaloo! I called out to one of the crouched neighbours on my way over to the bins. My absence would hardly be conspicuous anyway since it was going to be a big day in many places that day due to the fact that all kinds of events had been organised all over the country so that all sorts of people could discover and participate in the cultural life of their particular region. That being the case, since I appear to be a very culturally oriented sort of person, it is perfectly plausible that I was already under enormous pressure to negotiate a riveting panoply of worthy ventures further afield.

English, strictly speaking, is not my first language by the way. I haven't yet discovered what my first language is so for the time being I use English words in order to say things. I expect I will always have to do it that way; regrettably I don't think my first language can be written down at all. I'm not sure it can be made external you see. I think it has to stay where it is; simmering in the elastic gloom betwixt my flickering organs.

From the photographs it seems that it was open at one end. The other end might have been open too but the photographs were all taken from more or less the same position and so it is possible to ascertain the original condition of one end only and even then it is difficult to really know for sure what that dark space is, and going back through the photographs again did not make things any clearer. It doesn't matter very much. What the photographs all show over and over is quite plain—when they came here my cottage was just a pile of stones and a sprung tin roof. As a matter of fact I'd known about the photographs and other things right from the start—right from the time I moved in—and I think, at the start, I'd said something like yes, I'd love to see some photographs and read about the history of the place and, actually, I was quite sincere; at the start, when I first moved in, I was quite keen to see some photographs and find out about the history of the place. But I didn't follow up on the offer; sometimes I fully intended to, but I always forgot. We might talk for a long time, my landlady and I, about all sorts of things pertaining to the hereabouts, and afterwards I'd realise that once again I'd clean forgotten to say anything about wanting to see the photographs and historical records. And then, after several months of this, I had to acknowledge that the reason why I continued to forget to ask about the photographs and historical records was because I simply had no wish whatsoever to see them. Somehow the time for that had passed; it had passed rather quickly in fact. And then, when I was told all about the big day and all that it would involve, I felt deeply unsettled—and sort of angry actually. Why are they bringing all this up, I remember thinking, outraged. I was outraged in fact. Why are they bringing all this up? I don't understand the past—I don't understand the way the past is thought about, I don't know why but it makes me wild with anger, to hear the ways the past is thought about and made present. Enforced remembrance is, I think, a most stultifying thing. But then, as I have mentioned already, I am often alone and when I am alone it really is very difficult for me to gauge distance, and so, perhaps for that reason, I haven't acquired a particularly distinct sense of the past. I just didn't have the first clue about how to respond to any of this stuff if you must know because it seemed to me rather a peculiar way of coming at something that in any case still exists. In light of that I think it is quite understandable that my attitude towards the big day was of a fretful and somewhat indignant nature.

One morning when all this was just beginning the other one came over to me as I tightened the bungee cords on my bike rack and blithely informed me that my cottage had been more or less pulled from out the side of the hill. Did you know that, she said. Not really, I said. Which was quite accurate, because I didn't really know it, but I'd known it nonetheless. She beetled over to her car quite satisfied and I vaguely watched her drive off. The bungee cords on my bike rack were tidy and very secure now so I went into my cottage and put a clean sponge under the hot tap and held it there for longer than necessary because the fast hot water was very soothing on my notched fingers then I squeezed the sponge out a little bit and took it upstairs so I could clean a neat dollop of jam off of the bedsheet. Perhaps if I'd done this immediately after I'd got jam on the bedsheet the jam might have come off—as it was the jam didn't come off. The warm sponge was very effective at making the stickiness dissolve however so I was left with just a dark stain which didn't bother me actually, and as I looked at it it occurred to me that all bird shit is is jam really, with a little bit of white mixed in. It wasn't a particularly persuasive or significant idea but it cheered me up to imagine ashen professors stretching viscous strings of bird shit across thin slices of toast, which naturally they'd hold slightly higher than necessary between the pincers of their spindling waxen fingers, and I needed cheering up frankly because although I'd already known it I really didn't want to hear all about how my cottage had been pulled out of the side of a hill. It seemed an incredibly indecorous way of putting it and regrettably whenever I recall the phrase all I ever see is a glazed and gangly calf wrenched sideways from out its mother's dazed and quaking backside.

The large-scale changes in fact were of no interest to me at all; it was the small things that remained constant which sort of attracted me. For example, almost all the stones that make up the cottage are of an equal size and a similar shape—they are by no means uniform of course, but overall there is an impression of evenness and continuity. However, around the back of the cottage, up high on the left-hand side of the wall, there is an incongruously compact configuration of much smaller stones. And although this structural anomaly doesn't have the appearance of a flaw exactly there is certainly something antithetical about it and I remember that when I first saw it, coming back from the washing line one morning in June, it stopped me in my tracks. All the other stones mutely fulfil their remit you see, whereas this, this arresting convergence seems to be saying something—something I have not quite been able to work out, yet its errant poignancy manages to somehow transfix me nonetheless. And of course when I looked at the photographs from the nineties there it was, a little dimmer perhaps, but yes, there it was, in the photograph, as plain as day—and, strange to say, it rather disturbed me. I hadn't expected that, it seemed; I hadn't expected it to appear in a photograph like that. It looked odd and frightening, and sort of active. It looked like a concentration of captured faces.

Then, just two days before the big day, I bumped into a man in town who is the boyfriend of one of my neighbours. They can't get anyone to speak, he said. Who can't, I said. The girls can't, he said. Oh, I said, I thought the landlady's sister was going to speak. She was, he said, but she's changed her mind and they don't want to do it themselves. That's a shame, I said. You'd be very good at that, he said. I'm not doing it, I said. You'd be brilliant, he said. And what on earth would I talk about, I said. You've been there long enough, he said. Not really, I said, not when you think about it. Anyway, I said, it makes no difference—I'm not into it. Oh, he said, will you not be there on the day then? I don't think so, I said, there's so much on and I think I have to be somewhere else actually.

I love German by the way I really do—the sound—the sound of it I can overcome anything. Can see right through everything and overcome anything. I don't need to confide and I don't need to delve either—not at all. It all pretty well goes without saying. That's right, listening to German I can remain so private, so very very hush-hush—I can feel, really feel, every single one of my secrets, when I listen to German. It's as if they are buffed heirlooms—it's as if they are emeralds and opals and Japanese freshwater pearls! Berlin, you see, doesn't make things easy for you. If you want to get anywhere with Berlin you have to work at it; you have to slide down its walls a few times. And I remember suddenly what a sexy and beautiful thing it is to look at someone and decide suddenly and for no reason at all that I will for a while give them the cold shoulder. Of course it's expressive—what could be more arousing than inexplicable disdain my God.

The stones are not uniform of course and there are close-knit arrangements here and there of smaller stones which appear like the smaller fainter constellations one sees up above on a clear moonless night. That's how I'd begin. Indeed, I'd say, one's attention is drawn back to these gatherings of smaller stones in much the same way as the minor constella-tions beguile the stargazer, and perhaps for the same sorts of reasons—because of a seditious force which they themselves do not possess but which they serenely represent. These peering tributaries are in amongst the other stones and stars, but they are not quite of them, I'd continue, warming to my minacious theme. Why such an aberration occurs in the universal sky is a consummate mystery, consequently the wonder one experiences towards this most stellar intrigue is abstract and finds no foothold. It is natural therefore to return through the door unaccountably gratified and pick up where one left off—it does not unsettle you as does the hedged outburst of granite, which, after all, was put together by a bare pair of hands in the space of an afternoon. Again and again one's eyes return to it; these strange teeth, these melancholy prisoners, these motley iconoclasts, these en-compassed crones, there in the bedrock of all that is hefty and firm. And one registers, on the level of intuition, that it is impossible for anyone to make anything without mir-roring the nascent twist of cosmic upheaval. Yet it is but a commonplace to observe that every monument clenches the very element that will, eventually, overthrow it. Or perhaps, after all, the shapes of insurrection are only somewhere in my mind; a place that has become obscured in much the same way that the mounting formation of dissenting earth chuck is routinely concealed by the modifying application of concrete filler and whitewash. Pause. But there are gaps, of course. Here and there. Here and there there are gaps, of course. After all it is quite impossible to not let something in.

And I'd take a deep bow in order to fold up the elation that would surely come bursting out of me and then I'd straighten up, look very potent and solemn, and exit sudden as lightning with one magnificent stride and no doubt on the way back up to my cottage I'd see out the corner of my eye some skittered vagabond in velvet jacket surreptitiously pissing up against the side of the Portaloo. I saw no such thing of course: I stayed elsewhere and returned the following morning. Nobody was around, the girls had gone away in fact and so the balloons they'd tied to the trees stayed where they were and got smaller and colder and the Portaloo stayed put for almost a week. Once the Portaloo had been removed I took the scissors and cut down the small cold balloons. I left the bunting up because the bunting still flapped nicely now and then and I left the sign next to the pond for a long time because I thought perhaps they'd do something with it when they returned. I didn't know what exactly, paint over it and use it for something else maybe, but they did not use it for something else when they returned and it remained next to the pond for a long time and then, one afternoon, on my way to the compost bin, I put the bowl of potato peelings I held down on a rock and I went over to the sign. There were some slugs along the edges of it, and some wood lice too. It was completely soaked and the plywood was coming apart. Pond. I lifted it up carefully and carried it over to where the ivy grows round and round and jiggled it in behind the entwined trunk of a tree. It will surely outlive the pond in any case. It's not a very deep pond after all. I always believed they were endlessly deep. But when I took something down there one day that I needed to get rid of fast, a broken, precious thing, I dropped it into the water and it did not sink and go on sinking. It just sort of wedged itself and was horribly visible. And within moments lots of very small things, some of them creatures I suppose, collected and oscillated, slowly, along the smooth crevices of its broken precious parts.

Wishful Thinking

P ADS UPSTAIRS, scrapples about beneath ottoman, locates green flip-flop. Straightens, eyes bed. Thinks, hmmmm, stylish. Foxford blanket, textured cushions, suave bolster, a bit of broderie anglaise and so on. Then: have I had breakfast? Swiftly glances over the banister. Sees empty bowl and smeared spoon at the edge of the desk. Next to a bottle of Hawaiian Tropic. Factor 15. Thinks,

perhaps that was from another day.

A Little Before Seven

I WAS CLEANING OUT the fire grate first thing and as I dropped the pan vertical so that the ashes released into the bucket below I was distracted by an observation that was generally comical yet profoundly concerning: I rarely acquire any enthusiasm for the opposite sex outside of being drunk. It was soon obvious that this particular observation wasn't simply a fleeting instance of lighthearted self-derogation and as it achieved increasing firmness in my mind I felt incredulous and a bit put out that urgent tidings such as these could have remained distant for so long, since, it seemed to me, the instances upon which they derived foundation were surely not restricted to isolated and uncharacteristic phases, but more or less encompassed the entirety of my romantic career. At the same time I had to concede that up until recent times I'd been more or less drunk a good part of the time. Which meant, first of all, that a revelatory breakthrough such as the one I was presently undergoing had had, hitherto, no opportunity whatsoever to occur, and, secondly, it also implied I had, in all probability, been routinely duped by a compelling but ultimately fallacious string of attractions. So strange and inevitable was this thought that I turned away from it for a while and swept the floor, then, after a while, when I regarded it once more, it seemed to me suddenly flat and perfectly harmless, just like the sort of droll wisecrack one might see across those Technicolor postcards of sassy housewives wearing high-gloss palazzo pants in tropic shades of green. It doesn't mean anything, I thought, you're just going about a few tasks, amusing yourself as you go, don't give it another thought. Well that summation might be proportionate and sensible—and its recommendation workable—if I had in any way changed my ways, but, in truth, the behaviour upon which the original observation was based more or less persists—and I could not, with good conscience, continue to turn away from it.

WEEKS PASSED, however, before I took up with it again. Weeks, in fact, where I spent time with a man, sometimes in a state of inebriation, sometimes in a condition of sobriety, and, when I reflected upon this period of time, I had little option but to posit that, overall, relations with the man in question fared significantly better when I'd imbibed a little alcohol. Clearly I could underplay the unseemly implications of this bolt from the blue not a moment longer, and therefore took a little time, one particularly inclement afternoon, to ruminate upon it in a deliberate and dispassionate fashion—however, in truth, this levelheaded approach bulldozed my curiosity and stirred up nothing new to revive it. The premise just kept on repeating over in my mind like an appalling but dull diagnosis, and before very long I got up from my appointed seat next to the fire and went out the front to smoke a rolled cigarette and allow the many lovely things thereabouts to imbue upon my mind a more peaceable sequence of impressions. And then, just my luck, as I watched the branches of the beech trees being moved around by the wind, tossing out a few small birds here and there, a divination came to me with such blazing and spontaneous alacrity it pretty well blew my mind. However, the sensational mode by which the latest idea came to light was in fact not the least bit dazzling or unprompted but was rather the sort of consolidated outcome which is typically produced when a protracted and half-hearted analytical process aggravates the superior auspices of an exasperated subconscious. Consequently, the emanation's illuminating glare softened soon enough, enabling me to continue looking at the trees while at the same time according the contents of this most recent development a privileged yet manageable place among my thoughts. And so it was that I was able to approach its core without panic or distress, when either or both would have been quite permissible—and thus calmly confronted the nauseating possibility that perhaps the reason why I'd drunk so much for so long was because I enjoyed feeling enthusiastic about men and since that enthusiasm, which I so very much enjoyed, could not be brought about by any other means, I'd had no choice but to spend a good part of my time becoming drunk.

In many ways this aerated point of view appeared more troubling than the costive statement from which it had originated, and I was quite defeated in my efforts to distinguish anything amusing about it. In order to impart fully the seriousness of the situation I should make clear a distinction, and perhaps ought to have done so at some earlier juncture: I am not referring to the diffusion of those superficial inhibitions that may preclude one from being at ease with and enjoying the company of men in a recreational context. I have, in general, no inhibitions of this sort. In fact, from time to time, it has been pointed out to me, with varying degrees of justification and tact that I'd do well to cultivate a little more social reticence, sober or drunk. Indeed, regardless of how aggrandising it all feels from the inside, alcohol does not reliably enhance the most charming aspect of one's public arsenal—so, to clarify—it is not mere confidence and conviviality that is sought during these vital sessions of artful libation, but the stimulation of a rather more sophisticated piece of kit. Something that prevents one from scrutinising and dissecting everything that is said; something that shuts off the mounting dismay and stumbling evasions; something that enables me to hang off every word. A bespoke man-size filter for example, or a succession of perfectly pitched blind spots, or a persistent and delightful ringing in the ears, or a languorous crescendo of beatific bemusement. I don't know—whichever elusive device it is that surely one must have in spades so that critical indifference is converted, rather niftily, into mindless fascination, and one's usual agitation has the opportunity to metamorphose into a gloriously inappropriate and stupefying crush.

It might appear that this difficulty is merely circumstantial, relative to the second party in question, one that, as such, could be circumvented straightforwardly enough, were I to select to spend time with men who are in possession of qualities that are, in the most part, of an amenable and captivating nature. However, as tempting as it is to apportion blame, I'd be issuing an inadmissibly skewed overview of my encounters if I propounded the idea that, so far, I have not met with such men. I will not mislead myself or anyone else and pretend that I have not been acquainted with attentive, original and thrilling men. In fact, on the contrary, I have had the good luck to swing hands with some of the oddest males the species has to offer. And yet, how to reconcile such a fortunate and encouraging record with the aforementioned assertion that I was, in the most part, quite unable to endure advances made by any one of these extraordinary men until I had achieved a precise tone of inebriety?

THOUGHTS SUCH AS THESE lurched and abated throughout several afternoons of inclement weather and churning branches. In the mornings I did other things, and in the evenings perhaps I sat with a man and drank and got close to him, or didn't and became discomposed. On it goes. Essentially I cannot identify and fix upon a relatable purpose for them. That's what I've concluded and, in fact, from time to time, it has been pointed out to me, with varying degrees of infuriation and despair that I'd do well to cultivate a more conventionally orientated set of needs. Which always comes as a bit of a blow it must be said, because, on occasion, I have gone quite out of my mind with love, and yet, as it turns out, that isn't quite the same thing. But, tell me, what is one supposed to do exactly? Get cosy? Get cosy, perhaps? Get cosy! They stand there, you see, these terrifying and familiar entities. They stand at the door, a little before seven, with a bag containing God knows what. Some wine. Some flowers. Things like that. And I'll hear them coming. I'll hear the gravel, and when I hear the gravel I put myself in another room, the kitchen, the bathroom, sometimes, even, I'll put myself upstairs. I hear the gravel and the hook drop and the lower part of the door open and then, after a crumbling pause, footsteps, not many, over the stone floor. As this awful and accustomed entity makes its way in.

No, I'm not there, never there to greet him when he arrives. What does he look at while he stands waiting I wonder, and what thoughts pass through his mind? It is not immediately that he calls out to me and I cannot help but feel he must be looking at something and often the feeling that he is looking at something becomes so abrading I eventually tiptoe, lopsided, from out my hiding place. I come down the stairs or out of one of the adjacent rooms, always holding something, such as a towel. A towel, a newspaper I haven't been reading, a piece of laundry, a glass. Like something reclaimed and brought back from another world. And I don't stop. I pass right through and vanish into another part of the house. As if the item I'm holding needs to be presented somewhere as a matter of sacred urgency.

Such domestic fluttering is always interpreted as a cue, to move a little further in and set their bag of things upon a chair. I can hear it all from the kitchen; I almost always end up in the kitchen. Looking at the dishes and the knives in the plate rack, then down at the worktop, listening. Listening. In the kitchen, near the sink, some aspect of me is waning, and I cannot pin down exactly why. I feel utterly flimsy, yet I don't look in the mirror, nothing like that; I just stand for a moment, my back to the door and my tapering hands side by side on the worktop, pressing down. Pressing down with the concentrated effort of trying to give myself a little more density. I go to the doorway. I go to the window. I go to the entrance and push closed the top half of the door. And then I move across to the fireplace; sometimes I put both hands flat against the oak beam, and then I turn, and then I finally turn.

But no, that is not it. I appear to have turned but I have only twisted in fact; some of me has turned, and some of me has remained away. And yet it is an adequate gesture, enough to create a general impression of having turned fully and thus of being engaged and unopposed, even of enjoying the conversation perhaps. I do not have the courage to take the risk. To risk turning entirely and coming to face something very ordinary. I couldn't stand that so I stay twisted. And then I reach for my glass and I drink. I drink in order to—what?—become untwisted? Isn't that perfectly commonplace? Isn't that what's proverbially known as drinking to unwind? But no, that's not it. That's not it either. It's the location, actually—appearing to be located, to be precise—that's what I object to, and somehow wish to dispel. I want to shove the walls away and for the stone floor to turn to sand. I say such silly, merciless things indoors, the walls and floor and ceiling press so much acidic nonsense out of me— I become defensive, critical, intractable and remote. Impossible! No, there are times when men and women don't belong inside rooms.

We'd be better off silently overlapping each other; next

to a river or beneath the clouds or among the long grass—somewhere, anywhere, where something is moving. Isn't that right? Shouldn't we be somewhere where something is moving? It's the treacherous stillness I can't stand. When so much is at risk what sense can it make to be somewhere where apparently nothing is moving? There is music, of course, but selecting it is such a colossal anxiety—so often it comes out wrong and warps things, like a poison, casting me in some dimensionless and highly-strung role, an eternally spurned revenant in fact. Preposterous really, yet barely surprising. They sit there, you see, biding their time, these awful and accustomed entities, clueless, quite clueless anyhow, it seems, to the music, to the compressed hands and sipping breath, to the craning shadows. Perfectly composed and biding their time. Awaiting that kiss which somehow settles everything. And I have to try, so very hard, not to say something imploring and unsophisticated, such as: I only wish you could just spend five minutes beneath my skin and feel what it's like. Feel the savage swarming magic I feel. But an invitation of this sort achieves nothing, worse than nothing: it comes to them as a threat. A threat they scrapple to keep at bay by tethering worn-out schemes of placid cosiness about the place. They move about your home depositing things here and there, making ordinary noises along the way, like it's perfectly acceptable. It's ridiculous and quite untenable to become enraged and put off by such gentle armaments as these, yet I cannot settle, and so I drink. I drink to you; I drink to me. I drink to plough and fortify a one-track mind and suddenly, briefly, the blood surrenders, shuffles through the old channels, and there is no such thing as a false move.

To a God Unknown

A LEAF CAME IN through the window and dropped directly onto the water between my knees as I sat in the bath looking out. It was a thoroughly square window and I had it open completely, with the pane pushed right back against the wall. It was there, level with the rim of the bath—I didn't have to stretch or lean; it was almost as if I were in the coniferous tree that continued upwards, how tall. There was a storm, an old storm, going around and around the mountain, visiting the mountains again perhaps after who knows how long, trying to get somewhere, going nowhere.

And to begin with nothing, just a storm, nothing original, nothing I hadn't heard before. I went about my business for a while until it struck me I should disconnect the cables and thus the lights went out on those small matters I endeavour to attend to and I didn't mind very much because the matters were straightforward and already composed and yet were at the same time quite beyond me at that moment. It was of no great consequence really. I got into the water which had been waiting for some time, the temperature loosening, and then I had the idea about opening the window wide, which I did with no difficulty despite the rigid appearance of the clasp.

And then, from there, it was possible, unavoidable really, to listen to the storm going around and around, and I knew it was an old one that had come back—it seemed to know exactly where it was and there was such intimacy in its movement and in the sound it made as it went along and around and around. Yes, I thought, you know these mountains and the mountains are familiar with you also. No—it was not raging, it was not simply raging—I heard no element of anger in fact. How loud it was and yet so fragile, stopping and starting for a long time—it didn't know where to begin, but it was by no means frantic, either, not at all. I moved a web of lather about the roots of my hair and became immersed in the body of the storm; I knew its structure, saw its eyes, felt its past, and I empathised with its entreaty. It had style, it was experienced; and it came back, and it came back again.

Going around and around, trying to get somewhere, going nowhere. And even though the mountain did nothing the mountain was not impervious to the storm and in fact dreaded its retreat and longed for it always to come back, and to come back again. Then it turned in closer still and the rain came in slants through the wide-open window so I slipped further down into the clouded milky water and held my book way up. It was a book that made me long for men so so far away. The storm carried on into dusk and I stood in my bathrobe at the big window and held on to a cup and saucer with both hands. I knew exactly what was going on. I reconnected the lamps and eventually confronted the row of dresses that hung so very readily along the Japanese screen.

Two Weeks Since

WALKS UP BACK ROAD, holding on to hat, what he calls a skimmer, sees first one horse then another. Walks on. Climbs gate, jumps, lands wonky. Heart is huge. The lake captivates a loosening rain cloud.

THINKS OF TWILIGHT, privet hedges and a bookcase falling forward. Wishes for something. Raises hem out of the muck. Frayed lining drops, gets caught on a thorn, tears. Rain cloud pours down into the lake.

WALKS DOWN BACK ROAD, holding on to hat, what she calls a boater, sees the second horse first. White. A white horse standing, looks this way, then turns. Gave birth in the meantime. Blood fresh all the way down hind legs, cord hangs. A black foal slides about nearby, tiny forehead opening a warm pale star. Heart lengthens; cord swings.

Removes hat and whispers something. Whispers something again. Looks back, envies the deluge, moves into the long grass. Lets a van pass by.

Stir-fry

I JUST THREW MY DINNER in the bin. I knew as I was
making it I was going to do that,
  so I put in it all the things I never want to see again.

Finishing Touch

I THINK I'M GOING TO THROW a little party. A perfectly arranged but low-key soiree. I have so many glasses after all. And it is so nice in here, after all. And there'll be plenty of places for people to sit now that I've brought down the ottoman—and in fact if I came here for a party on the ottoman is exactly where I'd want to sit—I'd want to sit there, on the ottoman. But I suppose I'd arrive a little later on and somebody else would already be sitting upon the ottoman very comfortably, holding a full glass most likely and talking to someone standing up, someone also holding a full glass of wine, and so I would stand with my fingertips upright on a table perhaps, which wouldn't be so bad, and, anyway, people move about, but, all the same, I would not wish to make it very plain just how much I'd like to sit there, on the ottoman—I certainly wouldn't make a beeline for it!—no, I'd have to dawdle in and perch upon any number of places before I'd dare go near it, so that, when finally I did come to sit on the ottoman, it would appear perfectly natural, just as if I'd ended up there with no effort or design at all.

Howsoever, I am not, and never can be, a guest here, though in fact taking up the rugs and changing everything around and putting the glasses in a new place—two new places actually, there are that many glasses—does make it all quite new to me, and I have stood here and there sort of wondering what it was all for, all this rearranging, and it seems to me I must be very determined—it seems to me my mind is quite made up about who's in and who's out. With everything changed and in new places I can say to myself, no one has been here yet, not a soul—and now, I get a chance to choose, all over again—I must be very determined after all, to make things fresh and stay on guard this time. Yes, I get a chance to choose all over again, and so why not make use of such an opportunity in a very delightful way and throw a little party, because it is perfectly clear to me now who I will invite and who will not know a thing about it—until after perhaps, there might be some people who were not invited who might come to know a thing or two about it afterwards.

And that's just fine, that's fine by me. After all, isn't a

party a splendid thing not only because of the people there but also because of the people who aren't and who suppose they ought to be? No doubt about it, there'll be a moment, in the bathroom most likely—which will naturally exude an edgeless, living fragrance because of the flowers I picked earlier from the garden—when I feel quite triumphant for having developed the good sense at last to realise that people who are hell-bent upon getting to the bottom of you are not the sort you want around. This is my house—it doesn't have any curtains and half the time half the door is open, that's true. The neighbour's dog comes in, that's true too, and so do flies and bees, and even birds sometimes—but nobody ought to get the wrong idea—nobody ought to just turn up and stick a nose in! I wonder if it'll become wild or whether people will stay in range of tomorrow and leave all of a sudden around midnight. I wonder actually if anyone will ask what the party is for. Because of the summer I'll say. It's because of the summer—this house is very nice in the summer—and that'll be quite evident to anyone who asks. Yes! It's for the summer, I'll say, and that'll take care of it.

And sure enough there'll be martinis and Campari and champagne and bottle after bottle of something lovely from Vinsobres. And beautiful heaps of salad in huge beautiful bowls. Fennel and grapefruit and walnuts and feta cheese and all kinds of spread-eagled leaves basking in oil and vinegar. Because of the summer! Can't you see! No doubt there'll be some people who will be curious and will want to take a look upstairs—and perhaps I won't mind at all but I shan't go with them unless, unless—no, I shan't go with them no matter who they are. Sure, I'll say, over my shoulder, go on up and take a look. Be my guest. And, then, not long after they've come down and made this or that comment, I'll find some reason to go on up there myself—I won't be able to help myself—I'll want to try to see what it is they saw I suppose.

I wonder who out of everyone will sit on the ottoman? Well, if you must know, that is not a spontaneous point of curiosity and I don't wonder really because in fact I already possess a good idea—a clear picture actually—of who will sit upon the ottoman. Oh yes, a lovely picture as clear as can be. And as a matter of fact it might be the case that this vision preceded my fantasies about being a guest here myself and artlessly contriving to sit on the ottoman beneath the mirror—I'd go further and say the vision, the premonition if you will, of who exactly will sit on the ottoman very much instigated my fantasy of doing just the identical thing. What kind of a calamity would it now be if as it turned out the person I have very much in mind does not in fact sit upon the ottoman but leans in the doorway, for example? Just leans against the door frame and prods at the doorjamb, actually. Would it appear so very eccentric if I suggested to them that in fact the ottoman is a very nice place to sit? Well of course it would, it would be very eccentric, and my friend, and by the way I don't even have this woman's phone number, would understandably feel a little unnerved that I'd singled her out in this way—in this strangely intimate way. Of course I could devise some kind of game that included everybody and involved me appointing each person a place in the room—that could work—that would work—but it would be stupid, even if they thought it was sort of charming and zany I would know it was absolutely bogus and stupid, and how would I live with myself for the rest of the night after that exactly? Still, despite all that, despite how fraught this can all become, I am quite unperturbed—I'm determined you see, quite determined to host a low-key, but impeccably conceived, soiree.

I don't mind asking people to bring things by the way—and I'm very specific. Gone are the days when I make a lot of work for myself—that might surprise you, it surprises me. I'm very forthright on this matter, which is something people appreciate very much in fact because, naturally, people are short on time and they can't allocate time to trying to work things out like what to bring to other people's parties, it's a minefield, and even if you do have time to give to working such things out the fact is there is always an anxiety that what you finally select to bring is a real clanger. It never is a clanger, not really, but who wants to sit in the back of a cab with a bowl covered with tinfoil in their lap wondering if what it contains is going to be met with melodious condescension—who needs any of that? Give people a specific request and they arrive feeling pretty slick and raring to go. Not that the requests are issued in haphazard fashion of course—I know perfectly well who to ask to supply the cheese for example, and who to contribute the bread. It's easy to notice what people enjoy eating, and from there it's reasonable to infer that they'll endeavour to procure the finest examples of whatever comestible treat it is they have cultivated a particular fancy for. And, naturally, there'll be one or two you let off, simply because, gusto notwithstanding, they've never demonstrated any discriminating interest in what they eat. They'll probably rock up with hash and breadsticks, and quite possibly a dim jar of drilled-out green olives, and people who stay late will horse into the breadsticks and the following day there'll be shards of breadstick all over the floor, ground to a powder in places, where people have stood on the bigger shards while talking to people they don't usually talk to, or even when dancing about perhaps. I always enjoy the day after in fact. Slowly going over everything from the night before until it's all just so. Everything in its place: awakened, accomplished and vigilant.

As it turned out he came and she didn't. They couldn't get a babysitter you see. He came on his bicycle and his face was incredibly flushed, which he seemed to be enjoying very much. Indeed, it is nice to be flushed, whatever way it happens. I can't recall what he brought with him, which surprises me—I've a feeling it was something that needed to be kept flat because I seem to remember that the minute he came in the door he was anxious to look inside his rucksack. It was a tart, I remember now. That's right, he took a tarte normande from his rucksack and it was perfectly intact—and there was a bottle of Austrian white wine too with a distinctive neck which I put in the fridge right away and I don't think I opened it until much later on—the neck was distinctive you see and I remember putting my hand around it again quite late, it was really chilled, possibly too much. There was lots of wine, more than enough, and I was pleased about that, in addition my friend with tenure brought beer and a bottle of my favourite gin, which was unexpected and very kind because that particular gin is astronomically expensive. Everyone came with something thoughtful in fact and now and then I'd bring some chicken wings out of the kitchen, or one of those pizzas that have such beautifully thin bases some people presume they're homemade, and everyone already knew each other more or less so I could do whatever I liked and didn't have to worry about whether so-and-so was enjoying themselves because anytime I looked around there wasn't anyone who looked left out, but then it's so small in here it would be pretty difficult for anyone to look left out even if they felt it.

For a long time a man sat on the ottoman, I don't remember which man and perhaps it alternated. I just remember jeans and boots, and of course that wasn't at all what I'd had in mind. Quite often I'm terribly disappointed by how things turn out, but that's usually my own fault for the simple reason that I'm too quick to conclude that things have turned out as fully as it is possible for them to turn, when in fact, quite often, they are still on the turn and have some way to go until they have turned out completely. As my friend who lives nearby frequently reminds me, that part hasn't been revealed yet. My fascination was short-lived in any case, perhaps it lasted a fortnight, less, and it was only brought about in the first place by a blouse she wore one day—the collar, to be precise. The way her head was bowed, actually, just above the collar. So that I could see the roots of her hair, which was parted and pulled back. She was flipping through a very thick fashion magazine. One hand flipped through the magazine and the other hand was up near her face—near her chin—near her collar. What must it be like, I thought, to stand there like that, flipping through a fashion magazine? That shows you how determined I was, how utterly determined, to overhaul everything, to convince myself anything at all was possible—and obviously I must have thought that it must feel really terrific, standing there like that, flipping through a fashion magazine, wearing discreet earrings and a diaphanous collar.

Well really, I get so carried away.

The following day I took my time and returned everything gradually. There were lots of crackers and grapes left over, and some nicely slumped cheese. In fact I discovered all sorts of things here and there. Including a small bag of Jelly Babies on the windowsill. There's bed linen inside the ottoman by the way—some of which I've had for years.

Control Knobs

W HEN I MOVED IN HERE all three control knobs on the cooker were intact and working just fine. Three control knobs on a cooker probably doesn't sound like very many to most people because, nowadays, in addition to hardly anyone ever saying nowadays, very few people own what's known as a mini-kitchen, and those people who do are probably the same people who continue to unfurl the phrase nowadays. This domestic throwback comprises two electric rings, which are managed by the top and second control knobs, and an oven-grill, which is activated by the bottom control knob. Easy-peasy. I was informed when I first looked around the cottage that my culinary ambitions need not be in any way hampered by the diminutive dimensions of this appliance and naturally I believed my future landlady when she assured me she'd roasted whole legs of lamb in that oven for up to eleven people—however, I'd like to know where they all sat. I get the impression though that she prepared huge hearty spreads which were subsequently passed out through the window and taken off down the garden—I think outdoor feasting was the sort of thing that frequently went on here for a while. I have no complaints anyhow about the oven's performance; despite the fact that its wattage output is so modest it's a technical impossibility to switch on the larger ring when the oven or grill is in use, it generates a snug heat, and the meat is always impressively tender. In fact, in fairness to it, birds, shanks, potatoes, squash all do very nicely in there, and of course it's cheap, economical, to run. I've even got round its démodé appearance which smacks so unpleasantly of digs and hot knives; I've propped a mirror along the back edge of it so that now to all appearances it has four rings too, just like anyone else's hob. People said the mirror would get hot and crack and of course the mirror got very hot and cracked but once the glass had cracked three times it didn't crack again. Perhaps that was all the tension it had in it to be got rid of, because those three cracks occurred in quick succession right at the beginning and, as I've said, there's been not a splinter since.

I have never bought an oven and I don't know how long

one can expect an oven to keep going before the time has come to replace it but I'm beginning to suspect mine is very old and its days numbered. Not that there's anything wrong with it—it still functions very effectively in fact—the difficulty is with getting it to function; the control knobs are deteriorating you see. When the first one goes it's no big deal, it's easy enough to slide off one of the other control knobs connected to a part of the oven not in current use, but, when the second control knob split, things got trickier. Added to which, the remaining control knob is doing three times the work it used to so it is under considerable pressure and will itself fracture any minute I should think. It's a nuisance anyhow sliding the one remaining control knob back and forth between the three metal prongs—yet, as impracticable as it sounds, there is just no alternative way of turning them. Obviously I've attempted to twist the metal prongs with my bare hands, but they don't budge a millimetre.

I've been down to the last control knob for quite some time now, several months I should think, and it's only lately that I have begun to see that this deceptively trivial defect is in fact no minor thing. Full cognisance of how grave the consequences will be when it finally snaps was probably brought home to me by that book I read recently and the specific moment when the narrator realises she has only a thousand matches left. Actually I think there may have been more matches than that and the total was not a rounded estimate but a very precise figure on account of the fact the narrator had sat down at a table and counted out the matches carefully, one by one. This scenario might not sound like much of a catastrophe but in fact the woman slowly counting out matches is already negotiating a much bigger and completely silent catastrophe that has rendered her the last person left. Furthermore, it is not possible for her to wander wherever she likes to procure whatever she needs because of an invisible wall that occurred late one evening when she remained at the hunting lodge while her two friends went out to a restaurant. Everything on the other side of the invisible wall is, she discovers, completely motionless; birds, cats, people, her two friends, everyone—yet somehow a small area has been left out, which is where she is. And so she is the lone survivor of this impenetrable catastrophe, and has only a very restricted area within which to work out the rest of her existence.

She is not on her own entirely—straightaway in fact she encounters an animal which I took to be a cat for a long time until something was said about the creature which clearly indicated it was in fact a dog. I don't know how it was I came to make such an elementary mistake in the first place, never mind how I managed to maintain my misconception for quite so long, for several pages in fact, because when I looked back over those pages after my error had been exposed they offered such a tactile inventory of the animal's behaviour, attitudes and movements; characteristic details that are not at all in keeping with those one would typically associate with a cat. I'd been very engrossed with the book right from the start so it rather puzzled me that I'd slipped up like this and the only way I could account for it was to blame the animal's name, which was Lynx, which, as everybody knows, is a medium-sized species of wildcat. Well, it's no wonder, I thought, it's no wonder I took the creature to be a cat, with a name like that! But really, this explanation, reasonable as it is, did nothing to stymie my embarrassment since it implied my mind must be really quite feeble and literal that a mischievous bit of nomenclature managed to override pages of meticulous and animated description and impel such an unforgivable misreading. At the same time, one needs to be careful with names. Names in books are nearly always names from real life and so already the reader is bound to have some knowledge about a person with a particular name such as Miriam and even if that reader's mind is robust and adaptable some little thing about Miriam in real life will infiltrate Miriam in the book so that it doesn't matter how many times her earlobes are referred to as dainty and girlish in the reader's mind Miriam's earlobes are forever florid and pendulous. It is very difficult, I should think, to make up a person and have everyone reassemble him or her in just the way intended, without anything intervening, and sometimes, as I read, the pressure exerted by so much emphatic character exposition and plotted human endeavour becomes stifling and I have the horrible encroaching sensation that I'm getting everything all wrong or that I'm absolutely oblivious to something fairly accessible and very profound.

Needless to say since this particular novel is in fact the journal of the last person alive there are no other human characters in the book, which was a real treat, and I found it peculiar that somewhere on the sleeve, someone, an esteemed critic I gather, had described the book as dystopian fiction because it's not as if the woman's circumstances are portrayed apocalyptically and overall she does not suffer a great deal. That's not to say her predicament is construed romantically or becomes rarefied and nauseatingly didactic, not at all; this is very much a book about survival, and the grievous psychological ramifications and gruelling practical exigencies occasioned by confinement in this recently depopulated environment are in fact delineated with acuity and care. However, the profound existential and cosmological repercussions precipitated by such extraordinary isolation are also beautifully charted and it is quite impossible to stop reading because in a sense you want to go where she is going; you want to be undone in just the way she is being undone. Indeed, it is like a last daydream from childhood in many ways because hopefully the world for a child is mostly sticks and mountains and huge lone birds and as such almost all of childhood is taken up hopefully with just these kinds of boundless fantasies of danger and solitude.

Towards the first winter she has a cold for a few days and it really knocks the stuffing out of her. And when she is beginning to fill out again and feeling more like herself she takes a look in the mirror, which is quite a normal thing to do when one has been ill because there is a need to see if, in addition to feeling restored, one is also beginning to look like oneself again. However, it has been some time since she has looked in the mirror and so she doesn't quite know how to relate to or interpret the reflection she sees—it's as if she just can't work out what she's supposed to be looking at. Because there are no other human faces her own face has no currency and it doesn't seem to express any of the customary hallmarks and it's difficult for her to pinpoint anything in it that is familiar. Then, just as all this is beginning to freak her out, she realises that all the categories by which she has hitherto identified herself are now perfectly redundant. She is not a woman, though neither of course is she a man; she is more like an element. A physiological manifestation perhaps, in the same way the rocks and trees are physiological manifestations. Material. Matter. Stuff. For a few moments I looked away from the pages so that there was some opportunity for me to feel a little of what she must have felt when she looked at her face with the same sort of attention one brings to bear upon the bark of a tree, the surface of a rock, the skin of a peach, and in those few moments it was as if the pupils in my own eyes became tunnels and I was suddenly sucked backwards.

Of course, although she had outstripped ordinary ontological designations she had not completely transcended terrestrial binds—her life still depended upon the provision of warmth and nourishment and so practically all of her time was taken up with essential tasks like chopping wood, planting potatoes, milking the cow, repairing broken places and things, haymaking, finding berries—those kinds of tasks—and at some point I thought perhaps everything would be absolutely fine and she would just keep going. But this idea was only a brief fantasy really because in fact all the things she relied upon were finite and once they expired there would be no way of replacing or substituting them. Once all the bullets had been spent there would be no more deer meat, once the cow had died there would be no more milk and butter, once the candles were gone there would be no more light, and, once the matches were all burnt out, well there would be nothing really. And that is why she sat down with the remaining boxes, one afternoon, and counted all the matches out, carefully, one by one.

Paper, too, was also in limited supply, and in fact it seems she ran out of paper before any of the aforementioned necessities were used up and so the record of her experience ends before things get really severe and insurmountable for her. I think it rather shrewd of the author to leave a question over the precise circumstances of the woman's dying for the reason that it seems to me the woman's death wouldn't just have been about starving from hunger or freezing from cold, that probably it was about something much more, which cannot very well be put into such straightforward equations. Since her death is not dealt with in the book the only place it can occur is in my head, and I feel as though something is still haunting me or even that I am still haunting something, which means the book carries on beyond where it ends, and no doubt this was the author's absolute wish. It makes sense to suppose that since the underpinning of her existence had been totally reconfigured then death too would itself be an unexampled event; this was the proposition that slowly turned over and over in my thoughts as I stood on one leg in the bathroom yesterday evening, neatly clipping toenails into the sink. What exactly, I wondered, would death entail for her and how on earth could anyone even try to represent it? The walls and mirrors and the window were wet with condensation, and I was feeling really pampered and refreshed and quite safe when the images began to arrive. First of all I saw her melting quickly like the snow in cartoons, and then I saw her snapped up by the air and propelled as vapour fast through the spaces between the evergreen trees, then I heard her take a breath and hold it until it blasted her into little lines of fractured hoarfrost, then I heard her lie down on the real snow and the snow creaked and the blood that progressed through it shone red all around her settled body, then I saw the crows rise up from out of the highest branches and the deer lifted their chins and their eyes were completely black. I turned on the cold tap and watched the water swish away my surplus and I opened the window and didn't move. If we have lost the knack of living, I thought, it is a safe bet to presume we have forfeited the magic of dying.

Clearly, my predicament with the cooker is not quite as

dire as those redoubling aggravations that confronted the last woman left in the world, at the same time, once the final control knob splits and becomes useless, I will have no way at all of turning on any part of my mini-kitchen and so every known method of cooking food will be unavailable from that moment on. I have never had too much difficulty foreseeing impending setbacks and I have quite often identified the steps by which an oncoming obstacle might be avoided, yet it is a very rare occasion indeed when I've channelled any of this awareness into direct action and thereby altered the course of events so that they might progress more favourably. However, as I said, inspired perhaps by the book I'd just read, my musings on eventualities shifted out of an ineffective theoretical mode and I found myself taking a very practical view of the situation actually, which prompted me, first of all, to make a note of, and then carry out some research upon, the manufacturers of my decrepit cooking device.

Belling of course is the main exponent of mini-kitchens and I'm quite certain that when I lived in an attic near the hospital several years ago it was kitted out with a classic Belling model. Belling, by the way, is an English firm which makes complete sense to me because two-ring ovens are synonymous with bedsits and bedsits are quintessentially

English in the same way that B&Bs are evocative of a certain kind of grassroots Englishness. One thinks of unmarried people right away, bereft secretaries and threadbare caretakers, and of ironing boards with scorched striped covers forever standing next to the airing-cupboard door at the end of the hallway. And saucepans with those thin bases of course which burn so easily, and a stoutish figure probing back and forth in the effluvial steam with a long metal spoon. And laundry always, hanging off everything and retaining the shape always of those ongoing elbows and steadfast knees and dug-in heels. And coasters for some reason, and things from abroad, Malta for example, that were bought secondhand from somewhere close by, and a special rack for magazines and a special rack for ties. And nail scissors in the bathroom, poised on the same tile always, the same white tile like a compass needle always, always pointing the same way, always pointing towards the grizzled window. And extractor fans and skittish smoke alarms and bunged-up tin openers and melon scoops and packet soup, and a Baby Belling oven. You couldn't kill yourself with a Baby Belling I shouldn't think because as far as I know they are all powered by electricity and no doubt this specification was utterly deliberate because Belling would have been quite aware of the sorts of customers their product would invariably cater to and the sorts of morbid tendencies these people might brood over and wish to act upon and finally bring to completion.

In any case, gigantic joints of meat notwithstanding, there's not much room in a Baby Belling oven so I should think the possibility of comfortably shoving one's head into it is pretty slim.

I certainly couldn't get my head into my cooker without getting a lot of grease on the underside of my chin for example—and it stinks in there. It stinks of carbonization I suppose and that's only to be expected because I've never cleaned it out, not once; I just don't feel there's much point if you must know. It's not even a Belling, as it turns out; it's a Salton, whoever they are. The name strikes me as dubious—downright chimerical actually—and my hopes for acquiring replacement control knobs start to etiolate and turn prickly and I know, as I lift up the mirror so that I can get to the back of the oven and find the model number, that this oven doesn't really exist any longer and this is just a fat waste of time and the persistence with which I am trying to remain undaunted by these two facts means that either I am uncommonly desperate for a concrete diversion or that my blasé attitude towards most things is starting to make me feel sort of panicky and ought not be allowed free rein over nearly everything any longer. I make a note of the model number which is on a sticker, one corner of which is peeling away from the oven. There are bits attached to the underside of the label where it's come unstuck and on the place where it was which must mean there's still some stickiness in both areas and as such I wonder how they ever came apart. The number is something like 92711, but I don't suppose I remember exactly, probably the digits are prefixed by two capital letters, but I have no idea what they are either. This is not an occasion to formulate detailed and lasting memories. There are of course a number of regions in any abode that are foremost yet unreachable. Places, in other words, right under your nose which are routinely inundated with crumbs and smidgens and remains. And these ill-suited specks and veils and hairpins stay still and conspire in a way that is unpleasant to consider, and so one largely attempts to arrange one's awareness upon the immediate surfaces always and not let it drop into the ravines of smeared disarray everywhere between things. Where it would immediately alight upon the dreadful contents therein and deliver the entire catalogue to those parts of the imagination that will gladly make a lurid potion from goose fat and unrefined sea salt.

There were grains, of course. Grains and seeds, and a swan in fact. A tiny white swan, with beak and eyes hoisted as if regarding four or five swans walloping through the clouds above. Poor little white swan, so realistic and wistful, I'll put you back where you were. Which was, I believe, on the corner of the mirror frame. How did you get here little white swan? I turn you about between my thumb and forefinger and cannot remember for the life of me where you came from.

South Africa. South Africa! Can you believe it! It turns out my little stove comes all the way from an incredibly distant continent! I can see chickens with extraordinary manes stalking atop the flaking hob rings, pieces of caramelised corn wedged in the forks of their aristocratic claws. And all these big root vegetables with wrinkles and beards and startling fruits and rice hissing out the sack like rain. Everything red, everything yellow. I know nothing of course; I remember standing chopping vegetables for a salad in a kitchen in south London very many years ago and a man from South Africa stood beside me and showed me how to prepare the cucumber, that's all. I remember he scored the cold lustreless skin lengthways with a fork several times so that when he cut it at an angle there were these lovely elliptical loops of serrulated cucumber, and I have sliced it that way every time ever since. It looks particularly chichi in a short tumbler glass of botanical gin.

Dear Salton of South Africa my cooker is on its knees please help. Perhaps send the parts I need upon a cuckoo so they arrive in time for spring—on second thoughts a cuckoo is a flagrantly selfish creature so feel free to select a more suitably attuned carrier from another imminently migrating species—but please not a swallow because they don't get here until sometime in May, which will I fear be far too late, and anyway I'm sure they're far too dextrous and flash for such a quaint assignment. I live on the most westerly point of Europe, right next to the Atlantic Ocean in fact. The weather here is generally very bad, compared to the rest of Europe that is, and that might be a reason why not too many people live here. The fact that the population is quite low might in turn account for the fact that the country's basic infrastructure is very uneven which means, for example, that the public transport service is stunted, sporadic and comprehensively lousy. Fortunately despite all this, and its history of starvation which did in fact take many hundreds of lives hereabouts and beyond, the exact spot where I live is pleasant overall and taxi drivers often remark upon what an unexpected piece of paradise it is and how they never even knew it was here. I mention the famine, Salton, not in order to establish any sort of sociohistorical affinity which would be a very crass contrivance indeed, but simply because my mind is currently more susceptible to images of hunger than it has ever been on account of the fact that I am running out of matches, so to speak. This is not the time of year to be eating granola and salads and caper berries, let me tell you. Oh Salton of South Africa, do you even exist? I rather fear you do not, the attempts I made to discover your headquarters merely disclosed a host of online platforms from which hundreds of secondhand models are bought or exchanged. You are producing nothing new it seems, and are no longer on hand to assist with the upkeep of the kitchen devices you once put your illustrious and rather intimidating name to. No doubt I'll have to resort to clamps or something like that.

As a matter of fact I read somewhere that as many as two thousand stricken bodies were pulled out of ditches and piled onto carts then wheeled down the hill to the pit at the churchyard below. But I think to myself, not all of them were pulled out of the ditch. By the time they collapsed and dropped down dead into the ditch some of them would have had no form really, no flesh left at all. Nothing to keep the bones raised, nothing to keep the skin bound, and so the bones would slot down deep into the gaps and the skin would slacken and mingle with rainwater and sediment and the eyes would soon well up and come loose and sprout lichen and the fingernails would untether and stray and the hair would ooze upwards in rippling gelatinous ribbons and the teeth, already blackened and porous, would suck up against the sumptuous moss and babble and seethe. There would hardly be any trace of them, nothing to take hold of. Imagine that, Salton—already so wasted away there was nothing remaining to pull out and carry off.

Then I came across a company in England who supply spares, parts and accessories for all kitchen appliances, including the cooker, dishwasher, extractor hood, fridge and freezer. However, despite an impressively extensive catalogue of replacement cooker knobs my particular model is nowhere to be found in the existing options and elicits zero response when I enter it into the site's search facility and so the only remaining course of action is to fill out an enquiry form which I do because as far as I can see this is the end of the line and I may as well get to the end of the line and accept my inevitable defeat fully. Sure enough, approximately three hours later I receive an email from the company web support team informing me that unfortunately on this occasion they have been unable to find the item I require. They assure me that even though they haven't been able to deliver on this occasion they will continue to attempt to source the item—"If successful we will add it to our range and notify you at once"——I don't expect to ever hear from them again. I always knew, in the heart of my heart, I would not have any success whatsoever with locating replacement control knobs for my obsolete mini-kitchen.

I feel quite at a loss for about ten minutes and it's a sensation, I realise, that is not entirely dissimilar to indifference. So, naturally, I handle it rather well.

A WEEK OR SO before Christmas I was standing at the kitchen worktop in my friend who lives nearby's house, maybe we were sharing some kind of toasted snack, I don't remember——I was wearing a hat, I remember that, and perhaps I'd intended to go somewhere that day but due to some humdrum hindrance didn't really go anywhere. He was getting some things together but was attentive and forthcoming nonetheless. Because he works from home and his work involves materials and equipment and his home is quite small there is always a lot of stuff on the worktops and table and even across the sofa and often while we talk, I'll fiddle about with some item or other and may even pretend to steal it in a very bungled and obvious fashion. Oh I remember now. A few weeks before, he'd found a makeup bag in the road and he wondered if I wanted anything from it. That's not the reason I called on him though, as a matter of fact I'd seen him several times since he'd found the makeup bag and I'd almost clean forgotten about it but then, as I was coming out of his bathroom, I thought of it and asked him if he still had it. When I opened the makeup bag there was that deep-seated scent of sweet decay and the cosmetics inside were very cakey and dark. What's that, he said. Concealer, I said. And this, he said. I think that's a concealer too, I said. Do you think it belonged to someone older, he said. No I don't, I said, the opposite. How come, he said. Check out this lip gloss, I said. There was nothing in the makeup bag I wanted—bar a pair of tweezers. That's all you want, he said. Yeah, I said. Then we put everything back into it and he put the whole lot in the bin and then I noticed the pair of pliers on the side. Where did you get those, I said. You can have them if you want, he said. Can I, I said. You probably need it for your cooker, he said. Yeah, I do, I said, big-time. And I was about to reach for them when he said they needed sterilising first. Put them in boiling water for a few minutes, he said. What for, I said. They've been down the toilet, he said. And he wrapped them up in a clear plastic bag and I put them in my pocket, along with the expensive-looking tweezers. Give me a shout when you get back, I said. Might do, he said. Have a good one, I said.

By the way it turns out I depicted a number of things quite inaccurately when I was discussing that book about the woman who is the last person on earth—for example, the dog, Lynx, belonged to Hugo and Luise, the couple whose hunting lodge the woman was staying in when the catastrophe came about. The dog is actually a Bavarian bloodhound, which is more or less what I had in mind anyway, but he didn't just turn up, like I said, he and the woman already knew each other. There are other mistakes too, elisions mostly, but I'm not going to amend any more of them because in any case it's the impression that certain things made on me that I wanted to get across, not the occurrences themselves. Maybe if I'd had the book to hand at the time I would have checked the accuracy of those details I relayed, but perhaps not, at any rate it wasn't possible to check anything because I'd lent my copy of the book to a friend. My friend, who is a Swedish-speaking Finn, had been feeling unwell for some time and I thought this particular book would be the perfect book for a poorly person to read and when eventually I met her to collect it she put her whole hand on it very neatly and said it was an amazing book. We were both sitting at a small round table in the afternoon and we each had a glass of red wine. She had recently returned from Stockholm where she had been celebrating her mother's ninetieth birthday. She was feeling much better and talked excitedly about the trip—the hotel they stayed in, she told me, served breakfast until two o'clock in the afternoon! That's very civilised, I said. Yes, she said, and there were tables and tables of the most delicious things. Melons, she said. There's something from Stockholm inside the book for you, she said. Oh, I said, wow, and I carefully opened the book and inside was a tiny knife with a bone handle. That's beautiful, I said. I had to post it, she said. Oh yeah, I said, rotating the knife slowly. I like little knives, she said. Me too, I said.

The road home doesn't have any cat's eyes or stripes painted on it anywhere. There is no pavement and the cars go by too close and very fast. On either side of the road is the ditch, the hawthorn trees and any amount of household waste; including, actually, dumped electrical items. And as I walked from my friend nearby's house along that road towards home a week or so before Christmas I stood still at the usual place and experienced a sudden upsurge of many murky impressions and sensations that have lurched and congregated in the depths of me for quite some time. If you are not from a particular place the history of that particular place will dwell inside you differently to how it dwells within those people who are from that particular place. Your connection to certain events that define the history of a particular place is not straightforward because none of your ancestors were in any way involved in or affected by these events. You have no stories to relate and compare, you have no narrative to inherit and run with, and all the names are strange ones that mean nothing to you at all. And it's as if the history of a particular place knows all about this blankness you contain. Consequently if you are not from a particular place you will always be vulnerable for the reason that it doesn't matter how many years you have lived there you will never have a side of the story; nothing with which you can hold the full force of the history of a particular place at bay.

And so it comes at you directly, right through the softly padding soles of your feet, battering up throughout your body, before unpacking its clamouring store of images in the clear open spaces of your mind.

Opening out at last; out, out, out

And shimmered across the pale expanse of a flat defenceless sky.

ALL THE NAMES mean nothing to you, and your name means nothing to them.

Postcard

It is raining now and a bra strap has slipped down, which is perfect. The sound of the frogs now seems completely perfect at last. Like the sound of a vagina, because, after all, we would be cavorting now. It would be one of those times when I luxuriate completely and drew out everything—it is strange to absolutely know this, to feel this absolutely, and to do nothing but watch somehow as it goes by so very closely. The leg holes of my knickers are vacant on the floor right by the bed and I go on with finishing the Crémant. All the windows are open and all the shutters are folded back and I can hear the rain and I can hear the frogs of course—they don't sound much like you think they would, not at all—I would never have been able to find a way to explain to you this sound they are making—but now it is perfectly obvious, it is the sound of my vagina. God in heaven it is raining so hard now—straps are beautiful, just hanging in fact, off a chair by a pale unclean bathtub. It passed—I came off the bed and I walked to the window and blew two or three toe-nails out upon the wet roof of the very room where recently a dinner party to celebrate a birthday had occurred. The zip on my dress was long and gold, you see.

The Deepest Sea

THIS IS BEING WRITTEN with green ink—though in fact it is not, not yet. Quite some time has passed since this pen was last used—and, compared to the other fountain pen I have, which is used very often, it is indeed rather unwieldy—and perhaps for that reason alone I am finding it quite difficult to just get on with something.

It would seem the last time it was used the ink running from its nib was blue black. In fact it still contained the old cartridge, more or less empty, and I wonder—I can't help it—where all the ink from that cartridge went. Quite some time has passed you see since this pen was last used and actually I have a fair idea where most of the ink from that last cartridge went because the pen itself had been a gift as a matter of fact, and since there was a notebook along with it too it's reasonable to suppose that the two things combined, just in the way the person who made the gift had intended.

How very diligent of me.

Even now, this far in, the words here are still coming blue black—and give no indication of changing. Not so much as a hint, which I think is unusual. How can that be? I don't see anything odd or ridiculous about writing in green by the way; but, alas, it is not really something you can go on with once you've come across those unkind and boorish remarks and recognised the stigma attached, and then of course one just feels very embarrassed as if caught out and doesn't do it anymore and sort of pretends they never did. The reason why it's happening again now, or soon will be, is not because I have recently returned to green ink but because recently a cartridge of green ink was discovered in the bottom of a shopping bag I haven't used for a very long time. The reason I haven't used this particular shopping bag for a long time is because it has wheels, and while it was very useful to have a shopping bag with wheels when I lived in the city, it is completely impractical now that I no longer live in the city, and so the last time I used it was when I moved from the city and I filled it up with things from the kitchen cupboards in the house in the city I was moving from, and even then I didn't put it to its proper use and pull it along on its wheels from the house, a man carried it over his shoulder from the kitchen to a van that was quickly filling up with my stuff from the house I was moving away from in the city. Sure enough the shopping bag with wheels was stuffed with bubble wrap, which I'm sure I will need again one day, but I'm sure I don't need to hang on to this particular bundle, so I discarded the bubble wrap actually, and then, at the bottom of the bag, well not very much really.

A battery of course always a battery, a very small whisk, and a Sheaffer cartridge of green ink. I always assumed Sheaffer was Dutch or Danish or perhaps Swedish—who wouldn't? As it turns out Walter A. Sheaffer was born in Iowa and his fountain pens were incorporated in 1913, which means this year marks the 100-year anniversary of Sheaffer fountain pens and I'm sure there are some very fine special editions available to commemorate the occasion. Parker Pen, again to my surprise, was also founded by an American—Mr. George Safford Parker, in 1888, which means Parker are currently celebrating their 125th anniversary, in rather more understated fashion than Sheaffer I would think, whose current output is, in my opinion, a little ostentatious. Paper Mate, I believe, manufacture ballpoint pens—but that is not the overall reason why I have no interest in them and will say about them nothing further.

Time was I'd have any number of fountain pens on the go at the same time, but they were not interchangeable for the reason that they each contained a different coloured cartridge and therefore each had a specific and distinct function. I would negotiate both high-minded matters and bureaucratic downers with the steely blue black, flourish the gold for noteworthy turning points and milestones, and switch over to green perhaps for more clandestine dealings.

Yes, secretly, I wrote occasionally in green right up until quite some time ago—even after I learnt about the stigma associated with it—perhaps in fact I appreciated there being a stigma and felt duty bound to develop it further. Added to which my fountain pens were stolen—what I mean is, I stole them—quite easily—so that at all times I never had fewer than three fountain pens in the top outside pocket of my Crombie. I did not have the clips of the pen lids fastened over the pocket, ever, by the way. Certainly the tops of the pens were just about visible over the pocket but since that was just how it went I had no doubts whatsoever as to whether this was acceptable or not. In any case it was a particularly shabby coat, with a straggly length of thread where the top button should have been, and pockets that fell into the lining and a somewhat hardened hem, bent all out of shape, so really it would have been nigh on impossible to look highfalutin in it which was just as well because the last thing I ever wanted was to look highfalutin. I still have it in fact but in recent years it seems the only occasions I take to wearing it are when someone has done me a complicated and mostly unforeseen unkindness; it's a coat I can wear lying in the long grass with my arms folded even when the long grass is wet through you see.

I shall admit that I have always had an innate weakness for shabby clothes and so inured am I by now to holes and so on I have become quite impervious to the offense or alarm or unease or pity such thread-worn garbs might occasionally cause in others. I remember once years ago seeing a French girl in Dublin wearing a light coloured corduroy coat which had large stains down the front of it, on both sides of the zip, and the stains were very dark as if they had come from the pulp of a dark fruit such as a damson or perhaps some elderberries and when I was first introduced to this French girl with the filthy corduroy coat I couldn't take my eyes off these decadent blossoms of deepest crimson that thrived on both sides of the zip and whenever I met her on subsequent occasions I'd always feel a bit put out and slightly bored if she wasn't wearing it. I thought those stains were quite exquisite and exciting somehow—as if she were brandishing a glimpse of herself in process; they were so vivid and unashamed. Even now the ink has not changed and goes on and on blue black—I thought perhaps I was just seeing it all wrong so went over to the brightest lamp, there in the left window, and even there, there especially, the words are uniformly blue black, with no hint at all of green—not so much as a whisper.

Well I can't believe my eyes! I unscrewed the pen so as to check that what I'd put into it was what I thought I'd put into it, and yes, sure enough, there it was, quite quite green—and draining fast! A good fifth already spent and still no sign of it yet. The reason in the first place I came by this cartridge of unforthcoming green ink is because the shopping bag it was at the bottom of was itself out on the driveway quite suddenly, and without my say-so, along with some other bits and pieces of mine that are not in current use. Funnily enough I can't recall if I spotted my displaced belongings from somewhere outside or while standing at the kitchen sink doing the usual—furthermore, I did not feel any sort of anxiety or affront when, wherever it was I stood, I noticed some of my belongings had been shifted without my say-so from the outbuilding to the driveway.

Up until that moment I had more or less accepted that I was the sort of person who didn't feel at all easy about having any of her belongings interfered with—and by interfered with I mean anything so much as looked at actually. I'm terribly secretive you see so that kind of attention just doesn't suit me. Nevertheless, right there in front of me were many of my personal effects, moved by someone or other, quite suddenly, and without my say-so, yet I had half a mind to pretend I hadn't noticed a thing. So despite what I thought about myself it turned out my concern for these outlying possessions of mine was really quite scant and I think in all honesty the chief reason why I went out there at all was because I was wearing a new sweater.

There was in fact nothing at all untoward about parts of my stash being put out onto the driveway like this; my landlady and her sister have been making frequent visits recently and from what I have observed from the kitchen window they are very much taken up with putting things in order. Three days ago, for example, she came to my door and asked me about two large bags of empty bottles which have nothing to do with me, but of course one has to be very careful about how one communicates that something has nothing to do with one so as not to get the people it has everything to do with into hot water. And so now they've made a start on the outbuilding, and why not. After all it's become a dumping ground for every sort of discoloured tat, blighted clutter and things that are just too damn awkward to get rid of; it seems perfectly reasonable that they should wish to reinstate it as a repository for those things that aren't needed day-to-day yet can't quite be given up.

Indeed, when I first came here the outbuilding was like a sort of lumber room, and sometimes, when I was at a loose end, I'd go across and stand in its delicate gloom for a while and wait to see what caught my eye. And then, when I'd been living here a little longer, I might go ahead and pick something up and look at it that way, and then, when I'd begun to feel really quite at home, I'd occasionally appraise something or other rather favourably and thereupon take whatever it was back into the cottage with me. I won't go as far as to say the outbuilding contained unimagined treasures, indeed at first glance it all looked rather humdrum, nonetheless, for a while each time I went in there I wouldn't leave without bringing something back with me and I remember thinking what a soft touch I must be that even old things on a shelf can somehow win me over and impel me to return them to where they used to be. Because

I was quite aware that that was what I was doing; carting castaways right back to the very places they used to be.

We've been to the tip four times already, she told me, after saying something pleasant but slightly erroneous about my new jumper. We stood on the driveway and talked about stuff and the way it mounts up, and we talked a little bit about France and Italy—I must say she looked very well. Then we both went on over to the outbuilding where indeed more and more things had been piling up to the extent that it had become pretty well impossible to get the door open and I saw that in fact a considerable amount of stuff had already been got rid of or was out on the driveway in a kind of awkward limbo awaiting a final verdict and whatever remained had been stacked together very neatly, with my stereo as a rather impressive centrepiece. That doesn't work, I said, you can get rid of it. I saw my tent was there too—rolled into its proper bag—forming a sort of mantel, or lintel actually—and catching sight of my tent is always bracing and so there was no doubt at all in my mind about whether it was going or staying. Outside, on the other hand, were things that were not so easy to know what to do with—including, for example, many thousands of words I produced during the three years I spent working on a doctoral thesis. Many of the pages were loose and I knew very well they weren't in any order. There were quite a few of those frumpy ring binders that I could never quite bring myself to use because they are just so heart-sinking and severe and I recall I had to hunt high and low, which is actually quite a difficult activity to carry off in just two available stationery shops, for folders that were not black or red or blue. This is all a preamble really, of course it is, going on and on, as much as possible, so as not to ever get to what it was I really came across. There was an envelope, a white envelope— the sort which can easily accommodate an A4 sheet of paper or two if they've been neatly folded across-ways twice. And on the white envelope was somebody else's name crossed out and above that was my name and on the back was a small strip of sticking tape, that was still, actually, quite sticky, so I had to pull at it a bit in order to get the envelope opened. And there it was, from him, in my hand again.

It was my understanding that the letter had been in the house the whole time in the inner pocket of a clutch bag I no longer use, because that was in fact where it was kept for a long time, and I can't imagine what the reason for me moving it was at all. I had not anticipated standing with it today on the driveway, of course I hadn't, and so I stood on the driveway and just held it with both hands for a while, enjoying the occurrence of something I had not expected and feeling terrifically self-conscious in the process. I came right out of myself as a matter of fact; I could see my new sweater and the bright colours of its haphazard design, and I could even see around to the back of my neck and the loop of hair that had come loose from my ponytail and hung there. Then I realised I was waiting for the feelings to come; that same arrangement of feeling which always runs its course whenever I hold this envelope. But those feelings did not come, and, in any case, those feelings had never quite been natural—the fact that this letter existed at all was something of a miracle you see, there had been a great deal put in the way of it, it always felt so hot and vertiginous in my hands; nothing in relation to it could ever be fresh and voluntary. Yet that was all so far away now and today, this afternoon, the letter stood alone, unhindered, free from all the panic and recrimination that had followed and obscured it. I took it from its envelope and the feeling that came to me was that I was about to read something I had not read before.

The type was small and the font unfamiliar—the whole format was kind of strange actually—but I knew they were his words only, coming from him. And unlike those first times previously I did not plunge through it headlong but took it word by word, moving steadily, from one word to the next, without once slipping. Consequently every line I came across seemed different beneath my eyes—closer, much closer. Closer than how they had appeared to me the first times I'd read it years ago. Looking at it then with hungry rapid eyes I remember the same unconnected words would rear up forcing other words in between to recede and it was always as if I stood out on a small doweling perch above a loaded and churning landscape. I would see a thick black storm always, and colossal phosphorous waves, and amongst all the tumult and electric tints something firm yet recoiling would call out to me, but of course I could not hear what it was. And so I would just stand there, shaking perforce on my small doweling perch, feeling helpless and culpable and vicious for reasons I could not really examine nor wholly accept. Today on the driveway in my bold new sweater I went right along with him.

Word by word.

Step by step.

And directly came into contact with his mind in motion as it railed, proclaimed, recalled, confessed, imagined and eventually wrung itself out. Something was happening to him and what I held between both hands were indiscriminate workings out, notes that sought to give shape to a struggle: a love letter intent upon pushing right into every corrosive crevice and scabrous contour of its own impossibility. So much action, so much energy—so much of everything; I stopped and looked around, turning my head so as to include the gates in my survey—surely he was somewhere. All I'd required from his letter then were beautiful and accomplished sentiments not a pell-mell and furious thrashing out of his craving and cowardice. And yet it is that, the defeated aspect of desire, hopes dashed and ragged, which in the end outlives any exalted pronouncement striving towards the eternal; what I held in my hands felt so alive it seemed unthinkable that it did not prosper. Why does he not come through the trees right now?

I brought the letter back into the house with me but I did not return it to the clutch bag because it seemed to me it had spent enough time in there and belonged somewhere else now—though I'm not sure the new place I put it is an entirely satisfactory place. It might not be satisfactory, but it's certainly better than the clutch bag—to tell you the truth I was sick of it being in that clutch bag. It's an old-fashioned kind of bag, God only knows where I got it, a secondhand shop I should think, a long time ago: it's just the sort of bag a woman who's only ever received one letter in her whole life would keep that one letter in, and as a matter of fact I've received many letters, more or less consistently, starting from quite some time ago. Letters, poems, songs, cassette tapes, little portraits even—I even have an unremarkable pebble with a delightfully brazen message wrapped about it, I like that very much in fact; it always astonishes me. And all these notes and stones and so on are precious vestiges of something that took place and played out, however briefly, however blunderingly, and as such they are tucked in a big box all together, side by side, like lovely soft-hued sugared almonds, tied up with silver string. That's the difference. When, on the contrary, a letter attests to something that did not happen, that could not happen, it will not come to rest. It possesses you on and on and there is no final place for it. Everybody knows deep down that life is as much about the things that do not happen as the things that do and that's not something that ought to be glossed over or denied because without frustration there would hardly be any need to daydream. And daydreams return me to my original sense of things and I luxuriate in these fervid primary visions until I am entirely my unalloyed self again. So even though it sometimes feels as if one could just about die from disappointment I must concede that in fact in a rather perverse way it is precisely those things I did not get that are keeping me alive.

Sometimes I imagined us near the sea in a cove with the

tide coming in too fast. Other times we sat on great big rocks that struck out over a lake and we each held a bottle of beer loosely in our hands and we'd indicate things either on the lake's surface or right across on the other side with the neck of the beer bottle we each held loosely in our hands. And then, more and more, we'd be in a car heading down a long straight road with a beach just there to the right of us. There were lots of people on the beach and they were all incredibly fit and attractive in a florescent and bronzed sort of way—I wonder if we weren't in LA actually. Perhaps we were heading out of LA—I think that's more like it. The metallic sun was so dazzling I could hardly even see the bonnet of the car. It was beautiful. I looked down now and then at his hand and his lap. Then at his feet, the laces in his shoes in fact—and there it was, the only idea, the only thing I could think of: speed. Foot down, windows down; direct sunlight, all the way.

What we'd talk about is anyone's guess; I can't remember ever really talking to him. Except one day. One day we were talking, he was describing something to me, and one of the first words he used in his description was a term I did not really know the meaning of and even though I understood all the subsequent elucidations no picture could come together in my mind because of this one fundamental detail that I was largely unclear of. This made me shy and anxious because something was forming in my head regardless and I knew it was all wrong and I didn't want for anything connected with him to be inaccurate because I knew I'd only get to have one or two things about him to remember and so naturally I was very keen for those one or two things to be limpid and precise. What does that mean, I said. What does what mean, he said. Cantilevered, I said. Cantilevered, he said. Yes, I said, I don't know what it means really. And he explained to me what cantilevered means and it must have been that my face still looked concerned because he held his hand flat out in front of us and he took my hand and placed it vertically beneath his so that my fingertips connected with those little mounds where his own fingers began and, just like that, everything came together. That's it, he said, that's cantilevered. And of course the picture that fell into place only highlighted the life he had and the hopelessness of me supposing I could ever be a part of it. Even so, I loved the way he said it. Cantilevered. Cantilevered. I love the way he said that word. Cantilevered. I will never hear it and I will always hear it.

Oh, Tomato Puree!

Oh, Tomato Puree! When at last you occur to me it is as something profuse, fresh, and erupting. Alas, when I open the door and reach for you, the chill light comes on and shows you crumpled, cold, and, despite being well within your sell-by date, in dire need of coaxing.

Oh, Tomato Puree—let me lay you out and pummel those rigid furrows and creases! Reconnecting your fractured substance, so you might push aside the residue of previous abundance and come forth again, in all your kitsch and concentrated splendour.

Morning, 1908

SINCE HE'D ADVISED IT and it had immediately
appeared perfectly rational—to the point of being really
rather obvious—I filled a glass with tap water and took a few
sips. I imagine his idea was that I drink a full glass, but I just
wasn't able to stomach a full glass, not then. Nevertheless,
the little amount I did manage was really very refreshing—
uplifting actually—and the dizziness that had bristled in and
about my joints since I'd got up out of bed more or less sub-
sided directly after consuming it. That done, and better oriented, I took a long thin coat from the wardrobe, toppling a
patent leather boot from the shelf to the floor as I did so, and
put it on over my dressing gown and night slip. No one will
see me, I thought, but took a look in the mirror near the door
all the same. And was surprised to see that the three garments
layered this way looked very well, rather pretty actually, and

I evaluated, briefly, if I couldn't perhaps wear the ensemble publicly—on a Saturday, for example, when I go about my business, such as it is, in the town—before swiftly conceding that France, in fact, was just about the only place where I might feel comfortable in such an outfit, and on any given day.

This is my favourite time to leave the house and take a slow short walk. It is the time when my mind is least disposed towards fuss or hypothesis. It is the time when I have nothing to do after. Even so, I wasn't expecting much from it this evening—I don't know why. Possibly because I was taking one thing at a time and therefore such a thing as expectation was nigh on impossible to cultivate. Added to which, the impetus, really, for going out there at all was primarily to take some new air, and, secondly, to have my body undergo a little activity, however gently, however briefly. Pragmatic objectives, then, pertaining to my physical wellbeing, were my principal concern—I was not, for example, looking to overhaul my mental disposition or redirect my emotional bearings. To be perfectly honest I have, of late, become unusually disassociated from my immediate surroundings. The weather has not been particularly congenial this summer and such is my resignation that lately I have taken to commenting upon its brooding contrariety in routine phrases which demonstrate exasperation and contempt while leaving the utter indifference I've actually begun to feel towards it undetected and intact. It just never stops. Standing next to where the trees are particularly dense, long after the downpour has expired, you could be forgiven for believing it was still raining. But in fact what you are hearing is just the sound of detained raindrops, sliding off one leaf down to the next, and so on, from leaf to leaf to leaf, until falling, at last, from the final leaf to the ground.

Incredible, really. Or so it seemed to me as I went by and heard the thing play out. Further along there were those very small raindrops, droplets I suppose, which attach themselves with resolute but nonetheless ebullient regularity among the fronds of a beautiful type of delicate grass, appearing, for all the world, like a squandered chandelier dashing headlong down the hillside. I soon came to stand by one of the gates for a while, one I ordinarily pass by in fact—most times there's a wind blowing up here and regardless of its cardinal direction it invariably travels through the gate in such a way as to make a sound out if it. The same sound always. A sound I don't mind hearing incidentally, while passing by, but which would, I'm sure, induce a kind of peripheral insanity if attended to in stationary fashion for very long. Still, despite the gate being uncommonly mute, I would not describe the time I allotted to spend there as being altogether peaceful.

I'm used to vehicles coming up this way. That is something I am used to. And sometimes—though less often—they go down the way, and I'm used to that too. In either case I step into the long grass; out of the way. At such times, he, without fail, will put a hand up to the driver, whereas I never do—I don't know why and I do know why. I'm just the same, actually, when I'm on my own, but perhaps the reason why I don't put my hand up then is in any case quite different. Perhaps it would feel sneaky to do a thing without him that I do not do with him.

I don't know, and I don't believe unravelling these minor foibles is a relevant pursuit just now—the point is, no car came by. Not one, not in either direction. A car passing by me is something I am accustomed to: a young man passing by me on this road, on the other hand, is something I am not at all accustomed to. So it was that while I stood at the gate there came up the road not the thing I am accustomed to but its opposite, a young man, on foot, his head in a hood. An apparition quite without precedence—I saw him and I almost didn't believe my own eyes. I saw him, the young man, and it was an alarming thing. A most alarming thing that set my blood and organs into crashing disarray until I was soon drained of all former purpose, as slender as that was. Yet for all that it did not feel as if the alarm I was experiencing had originated from me—it was rather as if I were implementing the feeling for the purpose of some sort of nebulous external design. No, it didn't quite belong to me, and in fact it didn't quite belong to the situation either— as the young man came closer the disquieting sensation did not surge, as one would expect, but remained constant. As such I could only infer that the pervasive unrest I was under-going was probably not attributable to the young man's sud-den and unprecedented presence entirely.

I angled my elbows upon the gate's top railing so that my hands tilted back behind my ears and my fingers slid up into my hair, and I committed every strand and sinew to this position despite not being quite able to inhabit it fully. Ini-tially I thought such a posture might signal an impenetrable insularity—to the point of rendering me invisible perhaps— a somewhat far-fetched aspiration that was emphatically curtailed by the terrible recognition that actually I in fact appeared as defenceless and available for the taking as an ostracised vole. Unable to withstand or accommodate the panic that was the same but more exacting I found myself attempting to wrong-foot it with the speculation that perhaps the worst thing that could happen right now might not be quite as diabolical and frenzied as the thought of it jaggedly decreed. If it—that—were to happen right now, would it be so awful, I thought. Would it really be such an upheaval—such a defiling affront? Perhaps on the contrary it might actually seem fairly recreational, like the way dogs are, and not in the least bit vile. I looked as far into the distance as I could and after a moment of blank thought it occurred to me that I would very likely wet myself. That was a certainty, more or less, and it troubled me actually. The likelihood that I'd wet myself—not after, but during—troubled me. I surmised it would be unavoidable, really, because, for one thing, of all the rainwater that entwined in a lithe stream along the side of the road, which surely I would not be able to take my eyes off of, and, for another thing—though it's true I drank very little water before leaving the house earlier, I had in fact consumed a considerable quantity of ginger tea throughout the afternoon—consequently my bladder was already very susceptible.

What do you care, I thought, if you urinate on him during? Wouldn't it serve him right? I did not dwell upon the question long because the fact of the matter was that the possibility of urinating on him bothered me very much, and I did not, just then, wish to confront the reason why. As his proximity to me increased I became aware of myself from the young man's perspective—my shabby sealskin boots, the cerise snowflake pattern around the top of my thick Norwegian socks, the thin lace trim along the hem of my nightdress. My damp unbrushed hair. Nothing happened of course. I stood at a gate and a young man passed by. That was all.

THEN THE COWS went all queer on me. When I arrived at the gate, which was in fact a good while before I'd seen the young man, the cows scarpered off pronto to the left side of the field, down a kind of gradient—a reaction which, in itself, wasn't very remarkable so I accorded it no significance and mention it now only in order to clarify the herd's temperament and position so that the subsequent development, convoluted as it is, may be better appreciated. I didn't mind in the least that the cows took exception to my approach and found myself likening them to a shoal of fish on account of the way they each stared out at me from just one side of their head as they ran by. In fact, if anything, I rather approved of their taking up a more distant location since it meant my attention was free to overlook them. However, this pleasant reprieve did not last long. Soon after the young man had passed by me, and my hands had dropped down from behind my ears, the cows drew in close to one another and all looked up at me with the very same expression. I wondered what exactly they could see and did not move. Time passed, right up against me, and then the cows reeled forward ever so slightly—all of them still regarding me with that same expression.

The cows stopped and continued several times over and always in the same rhythm, and even though, as they got nearer, I felt increasingly aberrant, I managed, actually, to defend my position at the gate. In all this time they did not take their eyes away from me, and so unwavering was this confluence of looking that I went on wondering what exactly it was they could see. Once they got fairly close they became less unified—some were genuinely wary, while others dumbly followed suit, and at least one was acquiring that lurching confidence which menial and unexamined curiosity brings out in certain members of any species. I must admit that all this had me feeling fundamentally per-turbed in a way I could not describe or even classify. Did they know something? Could they see something? Were they waiting for something? What did they want, exactly? Despite my inadequate comprehension of the situation and the absurd tension that upheld it, it was somehow clear to me that something was going on and I continued to stand where I was and remained there until the one cow reached across the gate with her nostrils and eventually released a long sultry breath across the backs of both my hands—at which point I couldn't see that there was anything left to do. The situation, whatever it was, seemed at an end and so I stepped back from the gate, not quite ceremoniously, but with what I felt to be due consideration. Once I found myself to be very much back within the parallel parameters of the narrow road I shook my hair out a little and carried on up the hill.

It must have been the case that after the somewhat preternatural standoff with the cows I required a much vaster, more general, and completely disinterested picture to reassert itself because I began to extend a scoping look about me. A survey that might well have encompassed the broad and familiar panorama that is available from this vantage point had it not stalled upon the figure of the young man, who now stood facing northwest beneath the mast on top of the hill, his head perfectly bare.

There wasn't much opportunity this time to get worked up about his appearance because almost immediately I saw a line of smoke distended from his mouth and gave me to suspect he'd recently sustained some perennial and flawed grievance from someone close to him—a girlfriend, or his father—I couldn't quite make up my mind which. This sobering impression did much to humanise the young man of course, and so I continued up the incline with my recently re-harnessed equability quite uncompromised and the unchartered areas of my psyche hermetic and submerged. As I rounded the bend the atmosphere was very much involved in a customary process of change, and in fact some way past the Maamturks there was a sunset beginning. Beginning very ordinarily, it ought to be said, and then, via a series of protracted yet imperceptible increments, the sky imported the trenchant beauty and dubious brilliance of a new and unnamed world. And so it was I came to linger within the vicinity of another gate. I did not approach this one. There was no need. No need, now, to angle my elbows upon a gate and have my hands recline and disappear.

Everyone has seen a sunset—I will not attempt to describe the precise visual delineations of this one. Neither will I set down any of the things that scudded across my mind when the earth's trajectory became so discernibly and disarmingly attested to. Peculiar things, yet intimately familiar. Impressions of something I have not perhaps experienced directly. Memories I arrived with. Memories that snuck in and tucked up and live on within and throughout me. None of this distracted or deposed me, not in the least, I was still very much where I stood and it wasn't long I'd been standing there when I heard the young man walking the track that goes, more or less, from the mast down to a gate in the surrounding stone wall. I did not turn, but continued listening, waiting anxiously, I suppose, to hear the gate latch rise— because, as it turned out, I was not convinced that once he'd shut the gate behind him the young man would go right and carry on back down the hill, away from me.

I looked across to where some distant trees went black, and I looked at the mud and the rainwater that quaked minutely in the mud's depressions—there, directly, in front of my boots—then I stepped a little way forward so that my arms came to rest along the top rail of the gate. So be it, I thought. Let him come this way. It might in fact be the very reason why despite feeling the way you are feeling you were drawn out of your house this evening nonetheless. Wearing only your nightclothes beneath a long thin coat. It might, in fact, just be the very thing you need. Let him come this way. By this time I had no difficulty acknowledging that the shock and aversion that had coincided with his appearance on the road had not been incited by fear of him but rather by the horror I had felt towards my own twisted longing. A horror which had now more or less receded, along with all fleshly reticence. It might just feel like the most natural thing in the world, I thought.

The black trees

The tilting sphere

The humid bovine nostril

The sprawling chandelier

The thin lace trim

My damp unbrushed hair

All of them tangible and increscent coordinates in an immemorial routine of force and transmutation, of which the twilit taking of me was perhaps the final and most assuaging element. Surely we are all occasionally called upon to become a function of this overarching and irresolvable hunger. Who knows really what came over me—I was ill, after all—my defences were down, I wasn't quite myself; or, perhaps, I was myself more than ever. Perhaps I was stripped right down to my most vehement hidden currents: transparent and seen through, right there at the gate. On the way to the mast I met with my true body, dissolute and available—I saw it all, every aspect of its necromantic inclination—no, it was not fear that shook me, but rapture. Dissolute, truly dissolute. I heard the gate latch rise and I heard it fall back into place, and just like that something somewhere went slack and nothing further was issued. The gate closed and the young man turned right and made his way back down the hill. Away from me; head in hood, hands in pockets. It was as if the sifted moon, weak as chalk dust, had been abruptly discarded. Just for a moment everything gathered in dreadful suspension, my eyes gaped, cold and enormous—and then it all glided backwards into an atmosphere of broadening redundancy, intersected by a vertical and rather searing sense of abnegation.

Remote sensations really, hardly mine at all—nothing to take personally. Whatever singular intensity there had been sheepishly drifted off and the usual way of things resumed. I felt quite chilly in fact. The cows were still there by the gate as I walked on by, down the hill. I slowed down a little and thought of Jesus, I don't know why. Perhaps you all think I'm Jesus, I said, and then looked over at the windows of a neighbouring bungalow. A light came on. There were cactus plants in trays along the sill. Soon enough I was outside my own cottage, admiring its green door and deep-set windows. Fancy that, I thought. What a very lovely place to live. Then I arrived inside and after stepping out of my soaked boots I went across to the desk and began slowly skimming through a book of photographs by Clarence H. White.

The Gloves Are Off

WHEN MY FRIEND who lives nearby called over I was outside again on the steps this time taking the disposable barbeque I'd bought earlier in the day up to where there's a stone alcove—I was quite sure he wouldn't spot me straightaway and seeing oneself being looked for wrenches the heart oh ever so gently and must be one of my favourite occurrences—I thought I'd get to look at him lean his bicycle on mine, which was in the usual place, and go into my cottage, where of course he wouldn't find me. As it was he saw me immediately—before he'd even dismounted his bike—which rather spoiled things, and since I hadn't expected that at all I was caught somewhat off guard which I swiftly concealed by holding the disposable barbeque out vertically, right out in front of my face, a peculiar reflex which more or less pulled me together. What are you doing with that? he said—putting it somewhere, I said, and that's what I did.

He came on up the steps then and sat down on the stone alcove, near to where I'd put the disposable barbeque—we didn't say anything about it, perhaps because I'd already mentioned it on the phone earlier on, in which case he already knew I'd nothing yet to put on it so there was nothing much to say. He said he was fed up, or something like that, and I said I was too—he seemed to think it had to do with how the weather had been the same for two weeks. I was inclined to believe it had more to do with how our lives had been more or less the same for much longer. I really despise having thoughts like that since I can't ever reliably ascertain where it is exactly such ideas arise from, I didn't feel like going into it anyway and supposed neither of us would benefit from it very much even if I were to. We looked at a massive dragonfly for a while, it was very easy to follow because of how bright and big it was and I was as good as mounted between its perfectly Edwardian wings when my friend asked me to make him some coffee, which was fine by me and down I went. He came inside to drink it and I lolled against the wall by the window rather sulkily— it was too late in the day for me to have coffee you see, so I resorted to making marks on the wall with my irked fingers and flashed him sidelong glances now and then. He asked me if my water was hot and I said I didn't know, probably I said—his shower hadn't been fixed, which didn't surprise me in the least because when it stopped working before he didn't notify the landlord and I'm not sure what would have happened if he hadn't had an accident which meant I took care of things, including going around to his landlord and telling him about the shower and asking him to get a new sofa because the one that was there was old and lopsided and would probably be very bad for someone trying to heal a broken femur. Turn on the immersion, he said, which I did, and then I turned it off again and back on, then off, flipping the switch, on and off, on and off, on and on, and then I stopped and said now you don't know whether it's on or off do you, which cheered him up. It's on, he said, and he was quite right.

While my friend was having a nice shower I took the bowl down to the compost bin and it was comforting to see just my blanket on the washing line in the shade. The compost bin is really filling up and I couldn't get a good look at its contents like I customarily do because it's got very lively in there. There were just way too many flies this time, and I suppose now it'll only get busier and busier and some days I'll hardly want to turn and lift the lid at all. On the way back I put the empty bowl on the bench near the pond and sat down beside it. I think I should probably have just kept it in my hands really and held it in my lap because sitting next to the bowl felt really peculiar and it took some effort on my part not to glance down at it and ask it how it was doing. My neighbour's blanket was on that patch of ground nearest the pond where there is no grass just small stones, gravel I suppose, except I think gravel tends to make a noise and slide around a bit whereas this stuff is completely embedded and doesn't make any sound at all. Evidently my neighbour's blanket has been down on the ground for quite some time and throughout a lot of rainfall because it's practically enmeshing the stones and in fact in places it's difficult to tell the difference between the stones and the coarse and murky weave of the blanket, just lying there, like a flung-off reptilian carapace. The sight of it gave me the shivers actually and it was soon obvious that sitting on the bench was not very helpful and would improve nothing so I picked up the bowl and went on up the path towards my cottage. It was as if there was nothing left for me to see. I looked at all the leaves from last year on the main steps which lead up to the gate where the postbox perches and I don't know how many times now I've heard my landlady's sister comment upon them.

It's quite true; I don't do anything really. Any progressive human being with access to this much land would surely set about growing an impressive selection of vegetables right away. If I wasn't so lazy I could be enjoying delicious homegrown produce for months on end. It crosses my mind now and then of course; in spring the supermarkets have a habit of putting shelving units full of grow-your-own gardening kits right in front of the automatic doors, you can't miss them really, but in a strange way these packages deter rather than inspire me. They frequently have a lot of excessively cheerful writing on them and look so manufactured I just can't conceive how anything natural and enduring could possibly spring from them. Sometimes I've gone as far as to shove a beginner's pack into my basket but by the time I've reached the dairy section I've zero hope left that whatever it contains will amount to anything worthwhile so I take it out and dump it among the spot-lit "specialty" cheeses, which is probably very bad of me.

No weeding, no trimming, very little sweeping; when it comes to external upkeep I really am a relentless little lazy-bones. Though when the thatchers were here they left behind such a mess, and straw or reeds or whatever they are kept coming into the cottage, which made me so cross I had to get out there eventually and clear it up as best I could. My prolonged indolence in this case was I think quite reasonable since it mostly consisted of disappointment in fact. The thatchers arrived to do the roofs around the same time I'd begun painting over my bathroom walls which were dark green in the beginning, so dark and porous looking that sometimes at night their surfaces seemed to disappear completely and it was as if I might actually be able to glide my hands and arms and the rest of me far into the wall and enter some other place that probably requires small sharp weapons and a hunk of kick-ass cheese. However, after a shower, when there was condensation running all over them, it was quite a different story. It was a real little squelch hole then, and I often suspected newts and frogs and big-bellied spiders were peering at my dripping nakedness from behind the clammy glistening beams. The yellow I chose in order to give the walls a more respectable dimension was very smart indeed, what I consider to be a Renaissance yellow, or, if you prefer, matador yellow. I presented a sample to my landlady and she nestled it into her new handbag so she could take it to her sister who hadn't been feeling too well and they both agreed it was very striking. Imagine what it will look like with the grey slate floor, I said, and she agreed that it would look very stylish indeed with the grey slate floor. I got an enormous tub of it which was as well because

I had to apply endless coats in order to cover up that green which just seemed hell-bent on showing through and I didn't want so much as a trace of it remaining because of the beastly way it completely undermined the yellow and made it seem folksy and psychedelic, and of course that was not the effect I was after at all.

As might be expected I was in the bathroom all day every day for perhaps two weeks—I think I may have gone off somewhere for a few days before it was quite finished, so it could be that it was longer than two weeks even—and, naturally, given the odorous nature of my task I had the window open at all times. This meant I could keep a close eye on the thatchers, unbeknownst to them, and I often saw them gawking at one of the girls who was living in the main cottage at the time. I didn't find their smutty high jinks the least bit surprising and thought the way my neighbours made such a fuss over the thatchers really very misplaced and naive. They seemed to be out there every five minutes, taking photographs of the thatchers and with both hands bestowing upon them great big mugs of tea—as if they were dauntless chieftains from days of yore. I don't know why it is that people tend to assume that artisanal tradesmen who work with natural materials according to traditional methods are wholesome souls with salt-of-the-earth sensibilities.

These two, as far as I could see, were a right dirty pair and I seemed to be the only one who sensed it which was interesting for the reason that they spoke Irish all day long so I was also the only one who, strictly speaking, didn't have a clue what they were talking about. They came to the door one day with my landlady who wanted to talk to me about the struts, there on either side, which were in very bad shape apparently and needed replacing. After a bit my landlady leaned in and asked me what my Irish was like and the thatchers looked terribly pleased with themselves and began to chuckle. Well, I said, it's funny you should ask—it turns out I can understand quite a bit actually. Is that right, she said, and the two of them soon zipped up their triumphal tittering, needless to say. And what kind of nonsense would this pair be talking, she said. Oh I couldn't repeat it, I said, absolutely shocking—especially this one, I said, and nodded at the shorter one who went very red and slack and I knew he was as guilty as could be. They both shuffled about in the small space and began patting the shoddy struts with their hands while looking right up at the sky, as if it were the legs of a giraffe they stood between. Overall I had no truck with the thatchers—I hope you know what you're doing, I'd call up to them now and then, which delighted the taller one and completely mystified the shorter one. Indeed, it wasn't the crafty demeanour and furtive buffoonery of the thatchers that was a cause of disappointment to me; it was the origin of the materials they used to replenish the thatch that was the real letdown.

The reeds were in great big beautiful round bundles all across the driveway, and in the evening, before going home, the thatchers would cover them over so they'd stay snug and dry throughout the night. I'd inferred the reeds had been sourced from somewhere not too far away, along the River Shannon most likely, and that was something I liked to think about actually. I liked to think about all the little fishes that had nudged around and prodded at the reeds here and there. And I liked to think about the bigger fish, pike for example, that had occasionally swished past deep down and set them off nervously swaying, for miles and miles and miles perhaps. And the adrenalised coots spun out by the whirlpool of their own incessant rubbernecking and the hotheaded moorhens zigzagging to and fro. And the swans' flotilla nests resplendent with marbled eggs. And the sly-bones heron in a world of his own. And the skaters and the midges and the boatmen and the dragonflies and the snails and the spawn, and who knows what else the susurrant reeds are raided with. Are these reeds, I said to the taller one one day. They are, he said. Where they from, I said. Turkey, he said. Turkey, I said. That's right, he said. How come, I said. It's cheaper, he said. Really, I said. Because to tell you the truth I couldn't quite believe my ears and sometime later, weeks after in fact, I still wasn't convinced so I looked into the matter and almost immediately discovered that the Shannon River and the many tributaries that flow into it had indeed been a prime source of water reed until about twenty years ago. Since then widespread use of intensive farming methods has increased the use of fertilisers and these run down from the fields with the copious rain and contaminate the waterways so that while the nitrates force the reeds to grow fast and long they grow too fast and too long and so are actually quite brittle and pretty well useless and in fact wouldn't last very long at all upon a roof. And that's the reason why.

It seemed to me actually that it was high time I cleaned off the old leaves from the main steps so I went into the kitchen and got the broom and took it up to the top step. Now, I do not know if my method for clearing off the leaves was the best approach since it involved sweeping the leaves from the top step down to the next step and then sweeping both lots of leaves onto the following step, and so on. Probably it would have been better to have used a pan to collect the leaves from each step, but it wasn't that important to me to do it the best way and I quite liked how the heap spilled and prospered like a big tumbling ogre as I made my way down the steps with the broom. I was almost at the last step when my friend came out and just stood there. Did you have a nice shower, I said. Yeah, he said. About time, I said, and then I told him to go and get a wheelbarrow, which he didn't look altogether pleased about. Briefly I had thought that perhaps a little concerted effort might shake us out of our ennui but in this respect our natures are quite distinct and I knew he'd demonstrate no enthusiasm or initiative whatsoever so I gave up the idea that this might be an invigorating endeavour and simply continued to tell him what to do instead. I don't like gardening, he said, we're not gardening, I said. What are we doing then, he said. Tidying up, I said. Soon as that was done I nudged the broom over the large rock to loosen leaves caught up in a contorted tangle of grappling stems—what is this anyway, I said—it seemed dead, whatever it was, so I yanked at it until it leapt loose and the rock became completely clear and was something naked and impressive. I could tell my friend could see no point to what I was doing—I bundled what I'd ripped up into the wheelbarrow and told him to empty it then

I went off to find tools—he would be going soon and I wanted to know how it would be to go on doing what I was doing without anyone around.

I found secateurs and shears and since I was in the business of sprucing things up I was thrilled with both— particularly the secateurs because although I'd seen the shears here and there—in quite hazardous places it must be said— I hadn't known anything about the secateurs so they were a real bonus. There were a lot of rampant brambles, and other things on the wane. It had never before occurred to me to do anything about them, it didn't seem to be any of my business to tell you the truth—interfering is something I really loathe in almost all its applications. So, I was trimming—pruning you might call it—and pulling up weeds and patting the soil back down, and I soon felt like one of those ladies I'd see from the car window on the way to my grandparents' house with their ample backsides and baggy gardening gloves when I was much smaller. This is mindless, I thought, and very unflattering—stop it at once. But I didn't stop because I was so curious to find out what changed if I carried on. I had an uneasy relationship with my task, that is for sure, and I had to go on telling myself things like everything will grow back, it helps the little plants come forth, all the big stuff is almost dead anyway—

you don't ever have to do this again was the final assurance I offered myself—but if you don't do something today, now, how will you find anything out about how you feel? I couldn't continue with the tools so put them down and carried on with my hands, which were ungloved, and very soon they were stinging, which was fair. Come on then, I thought, and watched as my hands tore around indiscriminately. Is this kind of frenzied pulling and wrenching what happens once you begin? Perhaps I really hate all this stuff and it is a very normal and human thing to wish to crush it. But no, not that, I wasn't pitting myself against nature or anything as hammy as that—I was suddenly desperate to get rid of all this dishevelled foliage, it's true, but the reason I soon realised was because I wanted to get to bare soil—I missed it—it was all covered over and I wanted so much to push everything aside and see the earth. I'd had quite enough of leaves and flowers, all that rustling and blooming and liquid light, it was time for all that to pack itself off really. Except of course it doesn't go anywhere it just lies around like a lot of burst things and shrivels and withers and becomes very soggy and swamp-like. Oh, fuck the leaves and fuck the flowers! I want to see naked trees and hear the earth gasp and settle into a warm and tender mass of radiant darkness. I want to see the marks of hooves, not eleventh hour disposable barbeques. I want most of all to get inside there. That's right, that's always been true. It's the first thing I can remember. Standing at the back window, looking at the lawn, and knowing exactly everything beneath it and wanting to get back there. You don't know how passionate it is down there.

I believe that's where I lost my heart.

Out beyond and way back and further past that still. And such was it since. But after all appearances and some afternoons misspent it came to pass not all was done and over with. No, no. None shally shally on that here hill. Ah, but that was idle then and change was not an old hand. No, no. None shilly shilly on that here first rung. So, much girded and with new multitudes, a sun came purple and the hail turned in a year or two. And that was not all. No, no. None ganny ganny on that here moon loose. Turns were taken and time put in, so much heft and grimace, there, with callouses, all along the diagonal. Like no other time and the time taken back, that too like none other that can be compared to a bovine heap raising steam, or the eye-cast of a flailing comet. Back and forth, examining the egg spill and the cord fray and the clowning barnacle. And all day with no break to unwrap or unscrew or squint and flex or soak the brush. No, no. None flim flim on that here cavorting mainstay. From tree to tree and the pond there deepening and some small holes appearing and any number of cornstalks twisting into a thing far from corn. That being the case there was some wretched plotting, turned to stone, holding nothing. No, no. None rubby rubby on that here yardstick. Came then from the region of silt and aster, all along the horse trammel and fire velvet, first these sounds and then their makers. When passed betwixt and entered fully, pails were swung and notches considered. There was no light. No, none. None wzm wzm on that here piss crater. And it being the day, still considered. Oh, all things considered and not one mentioned, since all names had turned in and handed back. Knowing this the hounds disbanded and knowing that the ground muddled headstones and milestones and gallows and the almond-shaped buds of freshest honeysuckle. And among this chafing tumult fates were scrambled and mortality made untidy and pithy vows took themselves a breather. This being the way and irreversible homewards now was a lifted skeletal thing of the past, without due application or undue meaning. No, no. None shap shap on that here domicile shank. From right foot to left, first by the firs, then by the river, hung and loitered, and the blaze there slow to come. All night waking with no benefit of sleeping and the breath cranking and the heart-place levering and the kerosene pervading but failing to jerk a flame from out any one thing. No, none. None whoosh whoosh on that here burnished cunt. Oh, the earth, the earth and the women there, inside the simpering huts, stamped and spiritless, blowing on the coals. Not far away, but beyond the way of return.

Over & Done With

THE WINDS HEREABOUTS had worked up such a remarkable storm it made the news in the neighbouring country and so one morning I awoke to enquiries from my family, my father to be precise, about how I was faring. I said I was very snug indeed, which was no exaggeration, and I added that since my house is tucked into a hollow it is reasonably sheltered and altogether quite safe. Then I said sometimes I worried that a tree might fall upon it because I didn't want to reassure my father too much and thereby dispense with his concern entirely. I asked him of course what it was like there and he said it had just been very windy, just that. I've been up since five thirty, he said, which was no great surprise to either of us because his new children are supremely young and he told me in fact that the girl just then was eating a gingerbread man. Later on that day, or perhaps it was the following afternoon, I went out onto the driveway and not unlike the method by which an oyster-catcher grazes the shoreline I bent down here and there to collect the many sticks and branches that had broken off during the storm—which kept up, on and off, for about a week I should think.

Hard to tell this time of year how long anything is going on for and for that reason I took it upon myself to intervene now and then, such as when, just two days after Christmas, I avouched enough was enough and promptly took down the decorations. I didn't have a tree, just some things arranged along the mantel, holly and so on, but since it's a large mantel it is something of a feature and therefore very noticeable and I'd made it particularly resplendent and was first of all very pleased with how it all turned out. Even so, it quickly became oppressive actually and the holly itself almost sort of evil, poking at the room like that with its creepy way of making contact with the air, no I didn't like it one bit so a week went by and then it was all got rid of in a flash. The holly I flung directly into the fire beneath, and it was a young fire because this happened even before breakfast and as such the impatient stripling flames went crazy with the holly, consuming it so well, so pleasingly—I was enormously pleased in fact and shoved in branch after branch even though the flames were becoming really tall and very bright and the holly gasped and crackled so loudly. That's right, suffer, I thought, damn you to hell—and the flames sprouted upwards even taller and brighter and made the most splendid gleeful racket. Burn to death and damn you to hell and let every twisted noxious thing you pervaded the room with go along with you, and in fact as it went on burning I could feel the atmosphere brightening. I won't do it again, I thought, I won't have it in the house again. And I recalled the sluggish misgivings I'd felt when the man took the money out of my hand and held up a tethered bundle of muricated sprigs for me to somehow take hold of in return. Standing there, with this dreadful trident, while his young son manoeuvred a small hand around a grim bag of change. The whole thing was sullied and I remember at the time feeling faintly that I should just leave it but then I located the cause of that regrettably irresolute sensation to an area in me where snobbery and superstition overlap most abominably and I chided myself for being so affected and fey—what are you some sort of overstrung contessa, I thought—certainly not, then wish them well and get going. And off down the street I bobbed, yet, anachronistic feelings of pity and repulsion notwithstanding, I had a very clear sense of having succumbed to something I was not entirely at ease with and it was at that moment perhaps that the first pair of red eyes partly opened and considered me with age-old contempt.

The sticks, in case you wondered, make very good kindling of course and I thought it a good idea to collect a nice lot of them before any rain fell and made them damp and less inclined to combust. It was a nice thing to do anyway—going about the driveway like that, picking up sticks, was a nice thing to do. In I came, two or three times, and deposited bundles of sticks into the basket in front of the shorter bookcase. It surely was the afternoon by then and the atmosphere had really brightened, everything was good and nice again because of all that wonderful fluttering industriousness that keeps everything buoyant and encompassed. I'm referring primarily to the birds of course who had naturally always been there. During those two days that are decorously ceded to Christmas whenever I looked out at them it was not the same thing in the least as when I look at them on all the other days, and so, though I'd only done what I took to be the bare minimum, I acknowledged that I probably didn't ought to have gone along with the putative festivities at all this year, even to the slightest degree. And anyway, you do it or you don't—all I'd managed to bring about with my reluctant tinkering was a subtle yet agitating distortion. One has to have illustrated links with the fair to middling ranks of reality I should think in order for something like Christmas to really work out otherwise it just seems odd and sort of accusatory and one feels turbulent and extrinsic and can't wait for it all to slump backwards into its shambolic velvet envelope and shuffle off down the hill.

No doubt about it, Krampus was in tow this year, and when I looked at my lovely sticks piled so neatly in the basket in front of the shorter bookcase it seemed not for the first time something of a lapse indeed that I don't possess the first idea of how to go about casting a spell. Just say a few words, I said, as the sticks are burning, but that wouldn't be right at all and anyway what words would I say and I'm sure they should rhyme now and then at the very least and I'm hopeless at making up rhymes. It doesn't matter actually because it's all over with and there's no trace of anything now. Besides, there's never any need of course for me to be messing about with twigs and verses and chants on account of the fact that my technique for moving matters along is really quite advanced by now. I'm quite sophisticated in all sorts of ways you see and hardly ever need to dwell upon anything. That's right, I don't go into things too deeply any more—as such, when they ask, and they will ask, how it all went, and had I a nice day, I shall say it went just fine, thank you, I had a very lovely day indeed. On its own that's a little pacified perhaps and might well be considered evasive and could, thereby, be misconstrued, so I'll do my bit and say a few tantalising words about the dinner itself—we had pheasant, I'll say. One apiece. Wrapped in thick rivulets of streaky bacon and the whole thing gussied up with such deliciously tart and exuding redcurrants. Oh how nice, they'll say, was it nice? Oh yes, I'll say, it wasn't bad—tender overall, but perhaps a little dull in places. Is that so, they'll say, do you think you'd have it again? Sure, I'll say, sure I'll have it again. Though next time I'll do it slightly differently. Next time I'll break the bugger's backbone and do him in the pan.

Words Escape Me

SOMETHING CAME DOWN the chimney fast, swerved, hit off the coal bucket. A small thing, and sharp maybe—the sound it made when it hit off the bucket suggested it was a small sharp thing. I don't know where it landed, or if it even landed at all. I think it probably just disappeared. After hitting off the bucket I think it vanished, or was absorbed at least, withdrawn, anyhow, from all visible possibility. A little later, a long time after in fact, there was some thumping, as if inside—as if, again, there was something half-tucked inside the air perhaps. I didn't like it very much, the thumping, but this didn't develop into a difficulty for me because it too disappeared, or returned fully, whatever it was. I could hardly see by this time, my eyes were quite unable to focus—sort of unpractised and inept—as if they'd had no prior experience of form and perspective.

They just slid around, nothing was organised—it was difficult then to locate where I was, for the reason that I just wasn't able to establish any stable coordinates, so then I closed them. In an effort to attain some feeling akin to stillness I closed my eyes but this didn't alter anything, it was as if, in fact, they were still wide open. Indeed, I felt them to be open and alert and searching. They went on with their palpating activity for some time, sometimes I twitched—but not because I was asleep—I wasn't asleep. How could I have been? My blood was teeming, or ensorcelled, and my heart despised me, or wanted to divulge something, whichever either was at, the overall sensation was quite calamitous. I got that feeling again that I was some sort of funnel, for want of a better way of putting it—though a funnel isn't accurate at all actually since the direction is wrong. I didn't want to dwell on it anyhow, for the reason that that's precisely what it wants you to do. As much as possible I turned away from all that—I could hear the flames turning the logs white, a kind of tinkling sound, as made by icicles and Gothic snow.

I hadn't gone anywhere. Earlier I'd sat on the bed and faced the window. There was a male blackbird on the shed roof; his head was turned very much, so in fact it looked like he had shoulders. I think it may have been getting dark. That's right. I lay back then and carried on looking at the window, which was in a different place now, in relation to what it showed you of the outside I mean. Now the tree filled it entirely, not the whole tree, obviously, but that section where the tension between the aerial and the subterranean is most palpable and there are all these knots and orifices, and it could have all got a bit overwrought, one would have thought, if not for the occurrence of branches—and isn't it remarkable, and a bit repugnant, how the ivy always knows where the chaos is and wraps about it, siphoning off and getting greener with its potent volatility?

But such large beautiful impervious branches, they exceeded the window, and the sky appeared distantly available between them. I think the light was going, and I thought, soon that star from before will resurface—and that is exactly what happened actually. Just in the way I'd seen it. The sky was the darkest nearest blue then. At some point, I don't recall if it was before or after, I opened the top half of the front door and leant across the lower half. There was no rain now and I couldn't quite place when it was I'd last seen any but everything was soaking and dripping. I wished I could suck at something, it seemed like you ought to be able to—it was difficult, actually, to subdue the craving I experienced when I looked at the stones piled into a wall and the sopping moss spread across them. I don't know why I came to stop standing there and shut the door. Or maybe I didn't shut the door. That's more like it. I came to stop standing there, but I didn't shut the door because—I remember now—being at the desk—I was sitting actually, sitting at the desk—sitting and looking out—it's quite clear to me that that's how it was. And perhaps what I thought was, it all looks so very alive it might move—wouldn't that be right—it will all move down this way and come in through the door, and perhaps in through the windows too. Perhaps I thought something like that, sitting there, at the desk, looking up at the outside.

And perhaps it was the case that things did begin to move down this way, I don't know, but that was not the reason why I did in fact get up after some time and came to close the door. Or maybe it was, I don't remember in truth— I think actually I'd forgotten the reason that had caused me to open it in the first place and because I could not recall the reason for it being that way I could no longer see the point of it being open. I just no longer knew what the purpose of it being that way was. There were other things, after that—I moved around like this for hours in fact, liking the bathroom least of all, possibly due to its cotton buds and south-facing nozzles, who knows. There was no end to it really, not one I could fathom. I should have gone outside, but by now it was quite impossible—even in the dark. You're terrified, I thought, and you probably have been all day. What's all this been about if not panic? What other way is there of describing it? Terrified, absolutely terrified. That made sense, actually, and I felt a bit easier then, realising that. Then it occurred to me that perhaps I'd been terrified for longer than all day, and I had rather mixed feelings upon realising that—I wasn't much keen on the idea that I had been terrified for years, but it seemed possible. Well, I knew it really. I damn well knew it, have known it all along—and couldn't figure out what all this present fuss was about. Why it should be that my blood was rampant and my heart scouring for a way out. Why should it all be getting on top of me, as they say, on this particular day? I was suspicious really and thought it best to not get too involved with any ideas that came about, after all, being terrified seems quite normal, one learns to live with it—possibly you forget, or it tilts. And then, from time to time, such as today, it reappears, just to remind you, perhaps, what you are living with, even if you almost always forget. That seemed like a sensible explanation and I was quite satisfied with it, I didn't need to go any further. I thought again about that small sharp thing that had come down the chimney like a dragonfly first thing. And even though it was almost completely dark by now I opened a notebook by the fire and wrote some things down.

There were lines across the pages but they were imperceptible because of how dark it had become and once a word was written it was quite irretrievable, as if abducted. I went on, sinking words into the pages, perhaps wondering what or who was taking them in. And then, for the first time that day, just as it was ending, I knew where I was—I was beneath the ground. I was far beneath the ground at last, and my blood thronged and my heart flounced back and forth bewitchingly. The pen came to settle in the seam of my notebook. Sooner or later, I thought, you're going to have to speak up.

Lady of the House

Wow it's so still. Isn't it eerie. Oh yes. So calm. Everything's still. That's right. Look at the rowers—look at how fast the rowers are going. Ominous—yes, like the calm before the storm. If you like. Look at the rowers! Two long boats and bodies—rowers—like rungs or something. Like notches or rungs—or struts or bolts—something. The sound of the machine drying the bath mat behind me in front of you, very low—a good machine. Time to leave you to it pretty much. Handwriting, here and there—little notes, as you go along, things not to forget. They move me actually. Along with the photo on your travel pass, they move me.

I didn't put on my hat even though it's as cold as forever and the hat's right there in my bag at the bottom. My mascara came away in the night and for that hat to look any good requires a little recent eye adornment—I realise that. And I didn't say anything, not a word, about the creature beneath the water. No mention of the monster. The flowers are lovely instead, especially the roses. Oh yes, you say. They're high enough that I don't see Mary getting out of her car. I don't have to see her anymore, walking by and going into her house—it's nice actually.

Would it be a scaly monster with a tremendous tail, I wonder, or something wraithlike with straggly wings? Will it, in other words, be something dredged or something fallen? A decision doesn't fix because the day is actually more nuanced than at first appeared—and anyway I don't know where exactly but there is something shifting and suddenly the whole scene is quite altered. And yet, for all the world, it appears perfectly composed. As if hovering in fact. The whole vista hovers.

Some kind of trick obviously. I could remain like this all day I expect and not get any closer to working it out.

It wouldn't be a big deal—the monster's coming up from beneath wouldn't be a big show. If it went on behind anyone as they walked along the riverbank for example they might not even turn around. They could easily carry on walking in the direction of home and miss the whole thing. Actually for all they know this kind of thing is going on all the time just behind them without them noticing—though in some area of themselves they are aware, naturally, of what is going on—and this is why, from time to time, they behave in a way that, in the normal scheme of things, seems utterly irrational and unprovoked—because of this chimerically transcribed influence that they have zero conscious knowledge of. That could happen a lot I should think.

Up it would come, from beneath the water, of this you can be sure, without any ripple or wave. Just a little white showing. Air. Air tipping over in linked white collections.

I get so violently upset often. But now, look at this, not anymore. This morning everything is fine with me. I even stay after eating some toast, which broke up pretty badly into very unequal pieces when you tried to apply some cold butter to it.

There.

And without looking at me you put the knife down onto the draining board sort of immediately and you scooted off along the worktop to where the kettle is. I would have been exactly the same. I would have done exactly the same thing and in just the same way. I hate Mary's car by the way. I hate the cars your neighbours drive. All of them. What the fuck is it they are thinking of? Exactly? You have things like kitchen towels and coasters, and cats that aren't yours.

One of the cats walks with you up and down the drive—if the weather is good enough in the afternoon you walk up and down the drive. And you've got an electric blanket.

It had never before occurred to me that anyone might ever be afraid of me. And now, when I must accept that that is something somebody might in fact feel, I find it difficult to take seriously. For now it is all I can do to acknowledge the possibility—giving it credence is something that may or may not develop later. It's not angry I feel. I am not angry. It's easier for me to take a shower at home—which is still the case even when the immersion hasn't been switched on since yesterday morning so that the water won't be anywhere near warm enough for an hour at least. Maybe when I get home I won't have a shower anyhow. It doesn't bother me either way because I self-clean very well. As such, I don't know why, when I went into your bathroom to put my tights and knickers back on, I turned the knickers inside out. That's a new and very strange thing to do—I thought it at the time actually, as I was doing it, but I carried on anyway because perhaps I found it interesting or something. Perhaps I thought this deviation contained some sort of judicious insight. It seemed natural to go along with it— to not resist it, so, understandably, I wondered if it might lead to something—evolutionary passages have strange methods of harnessing palpability after all.

Nothing, anyway. Just an uncomfortable sense that my smell was being worn on the outside and smothered by tights. I look at but don't touch the earrings on the window-sill above the toilet cistern because I think maybe it will be nice if I leave them for you to notice later on, when you get back from shopping perhaps, or in the night, when you have got up to take a wee. What about this monster? Nothing more spectacular than a big bad-ass pike if you want to know. Shunting back and forth beneath the rowers, doing that shark thing with its eyes. That shark thing it learnt off the shark in the cartoon. So, in the end, here's a pike that imagines it's a shark. Leave it. I hate the colours of things today—the lack of deportment to be more accurate. Every-thing looks pissed upon. Like cats everywhere have just been endlessly pissing on everything all night. Drench-ing all the grasses and stone tracks and the leaves from every year that lie about. I hate cats if you want to know. I hate coming across photographic records of putatively out-landish cat behaviour and I hate hearing about cats. I hate hearing about how the cat walks with you, up and down the drive in the afternoons, when the weather is good enough—often the weather is not good enough. I sit in my place and look out at the weather and weigh it up too—and that's not as straightforward actually as might be supposed. Some days I think, no way, there'll be no walking up and down the driveway today—and then there comes a little light maybe, or, more likely, some sound, such as cows or birds—something really nice and uplifting, some indication that the world is really getting going again, despite the impression it tends to give. I don't mind the impression it ordinarily disseminates for the reason that I understand it— then again this is a somewhat curtailed claim because truth be told there does come a point when I hate its ongoing despondency so much. It's as if the sky some days is just hanging around. Moping—just moping. Moping and slouching and indolently seething. I'd like to shake it hard. Fuck you. Fuck you too. Man alive. Anyway, it was just a little idea, this monster. And now when I consider it that was the mistake, because if you want to know it started as an involuntary image—that was all. Just one of those visions that occur without prompting when your mind has retracted and is alert, or—the other way—when it spreads out and is almost completely oblivious. I can't be sure which state it was my mind was at when the monster came about—if I say the first I immediately know it is the other and then if I say the other it is obvious that in fact it was after all the first. What a lot of nonsense really, but then why on earth not spend some time in the evening this time of year trying to recover the landscape of some substratal figments? If you must know when we're side by side he and I rarely exchange any affiliated comments pertaining to our immediate surroundings. About what is actually right there in front of us—no, I don't suppose we ever occupy the same place at all. Side by side we're in completely different worlds. This then was a rare thing. To establish by empirical increments a shared perspective was a rare thing. So of course, when the monster came, all by itself, I almost shot a finger out excitedly towards it. Because, naturally, it seemed entirely possible—logical, actually—that the monster, in a different incarnation notwithstanding, had happened to him too.

Later on I cycle to the out-of-town supermarket and as I get onto the second road I notice that both cars which pass me in opposite directions have their lights switched on to the max. It seems darker here than it did two minutes ago outside my house when I was putting on my gloves and then sort of swiped at the bicycle saddle with my left elbow in an attempt to make it dry. I have no other choice but to turn around and go back for my body lights. It's a load of shit that

I didn't bring them with me—I even took them out of my rucksack to make more room for the groceries I was heading off to buy—what a load of shit. Where is my fucking sense of eventuality exactly? When I get out onto the second road a second time it's really obvious how quickly the last bit of light is getting used up, and of course there is so much rubbish all over the small fields I pedal alongside of. Entire household sacks filled completely up and knotted tightly and stowed into the back of the car just so and driven here. Not exactly spur of the minute then—but there's very little difficulty in rationalising the implementation of even very appalling activities. That's just something anyone can do very effectively and on the spot in fact. I notice the fullness of the moon when I come out of the supermarket—it's right there in front of me when the automatic doors retreat. The sky isn't yet black so the moon has a sovereignty it doesn't often possess—but in a way it looks as if it is coping with stage fright. Yes, it is as if the curtains have just opened on it! And so low is it that it seems only natural and forthright to reach out to the cowering moon. Pssst, take it easy, fix your gaze on something and get your balance, babyface— that's right, I'm bucking up the moon of all things—and yes, look, it's as if in fact the moon has closed its eyes and is taking a slow inhalation.

A deep breath before the rise and shine. I really want to communicate all of that, to tell you about the moon and its dithering autonomy and how I encourage it to get a grip and shape up, but I've already put my gloves back on and so I leave it, as inflexible as that seems, and when I get home, even though I take my gloves off right away, I don't text you immediately about the moon—I hang up some coats that were looking very untidy on the back of the armchairs and I light the fire and I take a bin liner from beneath the sink and dispose of some perishables that were left on the worktop and I go back outside to take the main shopping bag off of the back bike rack, and I think I also eat some cheese before I text you about the moon. As it turns out you're in the cinema so empathising with the moon's wincing fullness isn't on the cards for you at all right now. The moon of course will still be there, or thereabouts, when the movie has finished and you leave the cinema—but naturally I can't vouch for what condition it'll be in by then. The sky by then you see will undoubtedly be absolutely black—and a bit avuncular too I expect. It could actually get a little camp tonight if you ask me. Keeping the moon up with its camp and conspiratorial antics. Keeping the moon up all night long! Look at that, look at the moon yawning its head off all night long! You're not enjoying the film, in fact it's terrible, and I have a hunch which film it is and you ask me how I knew and I say I was talking about it in the week with a friend—which is true but doesn't answer your question—and I add that despite wearing gloves my hands got really cold while I cycled back from the supermarket. I was surprised actually, at just how cold my hands got, given that I was wearing gloves, and a little bit later on, while talking on the phone to my friend who lives nearby, I mentioned to him how cold my hands had been, despite my wearing gloves, and I asked him about a pair of thermal gloves a friend of ours had lent me and which I'd subsequently lent to him one evening. We'd made jokes about those gloves the evening I lent them to my friend for the reason that they are the sort of gloves you'd wear in Siberia and wasn't it just like our friend to have the sort of gloves you'd wear in Siberia, but now, since the wind is supposed to be coming more or less directly from Siberia, they are not quite so funny anymore.

I also watched a really terrible film, yet there was something so kindly about it that it was awhile before I could admit how awful it was, by which time its awfulness was somehow indivisible from its kindness, so I carried on with it, right up until the end—which of course I do not recall. Now and then throughout each thing that passes I see something like a lopsided Godzilla sticking up through the water—it's so revolting, the way my mind keeps on turning it over, trying to substantiate it. I must have really needed an idea to get hold of. I must have been really desperate to have something relatable to work with. Something with girth! Not a metaphor, nothing like that—I'd never want the monster to stand for something, that's for sure. At the very most I would have maybe said something about the house nearby, which, by the way, did seem a bit susceptible. Just having it in my field of vision felt uncomfortable if you want to know, as if I was a pent-up pervert in fact. Even looking away was calculated. Even looking away was looking. The first time I got home I turned on the immersion just like I knew I would, but I didn't take a shower, and even though I took my tango dress off and dropped it into the laundry basket I did not remove my undergarments so if you must know I'm still wearing tights and my knickers inside out. The smell of me like a young mouth to a compound fence. It's better anyhow to leave things alone. I've decided that once and for all. I don't want to be in the business of turning things into other things, it feels fatal for one reason. As if making the world smaller because of all the intact explanations that need to occur in order for one thing to become another thing. Secretly, deep inside, I accept I've no option but to retreat from a vocation I've never achieved any success from and my plan now is to fling in the towel and go to Brazilmysorebalimontanatrondheimnyonsbristol, as soon as my lease is up. And there's no fear of my lease being renewed by the way because my landlady has had to put all three cottages on the market.

She's more or less been forced to if you want to know. When she came around to tell me she was with her sister who was wearing a very peculiar hat with a wide furry brim which I couldn't deduce the point of at all. I hated the hat to be perfectly blunt, and I also hated, maybe even more than the hat, the pale frosty lipstick she had selected to wear. Whatever was the point of all that? Exactly? She kept looking down at some metal things I have resting near my door and then back up at me as if all of this was a question I would feel pressed to answer, but I easily ignored her and asked my landlady how she felt about having to sell. I could sense her response was regrettably hampered by the presence of her sister and the impatient brim of her peculiar furry hat, which took up a lot of space actually so that it was quite a job for the pair of them to stand side by side in my doorway. She said it would be ages yet before anything happened, and in any case they'd have to give me two months' notice because of how long I'd been living here and I said that was just fine. As a matter of fact, I've been thinking about taking off somewhere I said. Is that right, she said, anywhere in mind? Oh, Brazil, I said. Brazil, she said. My landlady's hands were very apparent for some reason and in order to stop looking at her fingers especially I found I looked down at my own hands, which upset me very much actually, so I said that's fine again and keep me posted then I went into the kitchen, and not long after, while I stood at my kitchen sink swilling out the teapot, two men arrived who I presume were estate agents because of the kind of folders they waved about and did nothing with.

It's a devil to know what to take seriously.

I don't know why it was I got talking about Martin's Hill like that—I don't know what exactly I was getting at with that little reverie on the arm of the armchair this morning. Has it really become an inclination of mine to reminisce in such a gratuitous way? And since when? Because if you must know I don't recall ever regarding anything I may remember from my past as being particularly interesting or poignant, or even especially reliable actually. On account of my radical immaturity—characterised by a persistent lack of ambition—real events don't make much difference to me, as such the impact they have upon my mind is either zilch or blistering, and so, naturally, I have to question my facility to form memories that have any congruity at all with what in fact took place—landmark events and so on included. Having said that my dreams demonstrate a rather impressive mnemonic flair—I don't dream about the past, not the outside past, but quite often I will dream about, for example, daydreams I had when I was much younger—beside trees, behind curtains, that kind of thing. You see? Even so—despite my generally dubious mode of relation—I seemed rather determined to make something out of Martin's Hill.

It might be the case that I thought my somewhat poeti-cised rendering of its central catastrophe made me sound perspicacious and grown-up, and very aware of how one's life develops according to the uncanny distillation of subtle kairotic shifts. As a rule of thumb I don't have much enthu-siasm for inventorial reflection, however, on this occasion I transgressed my thumb multiple times—I even went so far as to say we had chicken. Now, I can't be sure at all that we had chicken. It's very likely we had chicken because it hap-pened in the mid-nineties and everyone knows that a staple component of an English picnic in the mid-nineties was cold roasted chicken, along with some sort of pasta salad, and French bread and satsumas, and a six-pack of chocolate mini-rolls. Martin's Hill of all things! Oh yes, I really went into some detail and highlighted quite the prelapsarian scene this morning after broken toast while prodding the arm of the armchair with my pernickety sit bones his head more or less beneath my chin both looking out right across everything. The lake, the river, the ruined castle, the shrubs, the tall trees, the dismal clouds, the pissed-upon reeds, the rowers and their boats, the monster, the house nearby, the children, their mother, the garage, the garden tools, the drying clods, the hallway, the stairs, the doors, the keyholes, the bed, the underneath, the terror, the cold floor, the ankle-straps, the perpetuating dust. And one side of Martin's Hill was very steep, I explained—I think I may have used the word gradient if you want to know—and I think my brother's ball must have rolled down it you see, there must have been something anyway that lured him to that side of the hill because you wouldn't normally go that side ever—it was very steep you see, and overgrown—steep, uneven and overgrown. Orange. Blue. Orange. Blue. Orange. And he was all right for the first few steps, then he couldn't keep pace—he lost control and he fell actually. Fell all the way down to the bottom of Martin's Hill. All on his own with me just looking, and there was the proof I suppose that I was older at last.

I hated feeling that actually yet it was sort of attenuated by the anticipation I had towards the evening to come and didn't those two sensations, first loss and high hopes, combine to produce possibly my initial experience of melancholia. And didn't I immediately discover that melancholia brought something out in me that felt more authentic and effortless than anything I'd previously alchemised.

Look here, it's perfectly obvious by now to anyone that my head is turned by imagined elsewheres and hardly at all by present circumstances—even so no one can know what trip is going on and on in anyone else's mind and so, for that reason solely perhaps, the way I go about my business, such as it is, can be very confusing, bewildering, unaccountable—even, actually, offensive sometimes. It's easy to be suspicious of a drifter like me and it frequently happens that I am accused of all sorts of impertinence. This time last year for example someone I know in a sort of professional way arranged to meet me in a hotel conservatory around lunchtime purely for the purpose of relaying an unflattering compendium of controvertible opinions pertaining to my character and outlook—an apocryphal catalogue of puerile anecdotes, which, by the way, he'd quite obviously had some assistance piecing together—and all this for my own good apparently! Well let me tell you I found the whole ordeal very off-putting and I had no instinctive way of responding to it—it was just about beyond me. We'd ordered buns and the buns were on the coffee table and there were those stupid fruitless cartons of vapid jam I hate so much next to the buns. I tried to be gracious, be gracious, I thought, but that was a confounding prescription for the reason that I could not at all determine whom out of the two of us I should be gracious to.

It was very disturbing actually and it wasn't until after I'd talked it over with a friend in her car on my driveway a few times that I felt sure enough of myself to not give two hoots about it anymore. It's all by-the-by now. Under the bridge and so on. Since we are going on a two-day outing tomorrow I brought the phone down to the garden after lunch and called him so we could discuss arrangements. He was eating soup if you want to know. Tomato soup with a drop of milk stirred in. He asked me right at the start of the phone call if I'd mind him eating his soup while we talked and I said I didn't know, maybe I would mind, it depended on how much noise he made. I was teasing, of course, that had been the intention anyhow, but as it turned out there was also a trace of sincerity in my voice, which took me by surprise actually—I quickly counteracted this unattractive flash of knee-jerk resistance by laughing a little, which was very relaxing of course, and then I invited him to go right ahead and eat the soup.

Because it had been established he was eating soup we talked for a little while about soup—he eats soup almost every day whereas I seldom bother with it and it was actually as if he needed to somehow reconcile this difference, or at least understand it better. When he surmises that I don't like soup I find I'm reluctant to agree—I do like soup very much in fact, but I don't enjoy the process of eating it—all that lifting and lowering of the spoon over and over, it soon gets very tedious, so mechanical—no, it's the dismal activity of eating soup that turns me off, not the taste. I'm rolling about on my sleeping bag near the washing line while these disparities are addressed—the weather has been so good the last two days I took the opportunity to wash blankets and cushion covers and small rugs. I tell him about the cycle I went for last night, how beautiful it was because of the way the lanes were moonlit. I told him I got upset and pissed off because of a dog that ran out at me and went on barking at my ankles even as my legs lost density and the pedals spun uselessly beneath their sudden cascade. He told me I should bring a stick with me so in future I can belt dogs like that across the head and I point out that it might be difficult to take a stick on a bike and he says I'd figure it out. You need it, he says. Your shirts dried nicely I say, I'll iron them a bit later—do you want me to bring both tomorrow? Yes, he says, bring them both. You'll need another one, I say. Yes, he says, the one I'm wearing. Which one is that, I ask. I don't know yet, he says. Oh, I say, you mean the one you'll be wearing tomorrow—not now. Why don't you wear the blue linen one, I say. The one with spots on, he says. Yes, I say—even though they're not spots, they're very small flowers. Okay, he says, I'll wear it with the navy jumper. You look nice in that, I say. Then, at the end of the phone call, he reveals that he's been holding the soup bowl and drinking from it with one hand and holding his mobile and talking to me with the other the whole time.

You know, he says, if you were to drink soup like I'm doing now you wouldn't have to worry about a spoon and you could enjoy it better.

To be honest I think I may have already experimented with taking soup directly from the bowl but as it turned out it wasn't a practice I was particularly comfortable with adopting for the reason that it felt actually as if I was pretending to be from somewhere I'm not—I don't know where, another continent, another epoch possibly—it hardly matters—it's the sensation that's relevant and the sensation, above all else, was one of displacement. Strange really. Besides which I often drink coffee from a small noodle-bowl and that just suits me fine if you want to know. I've four small noodle-bowls and it works out well with each, the terracotta one especially. And the green of course. I struggle to savour tea drunk out of anything that isn't white and chipped in the right place—and that's still unwavering even though I drink it black now. When I was at school I was friends with a girl whose mother had no idea really when it came to housekeeping, the kitchen was especially unpleasant—deathly in fact. She had some pretty morbid ideas you see, such as storing teddy bears and owls in the freezer chest. Can you imagine? Fascinating really. From time to time she made efforts to introduce some warmth to the place, efforts that were so negligible that there was often something very untoward about the incongruous items they found expression through—embossed hand towels for one, and patterned mugs for another. Now, I'd already come across patterned mugs and as such was quite familiar with the concept—and although not preferable very occasionally they are perfectly passable. Nothing like these though—these were quite shuddersome on account of the pattern not being limited to the outside of the mug—as incredible as it sounds a single motif was discoverable on the inside of the mug too. She thought that was great, I remember very well her making a point of showing it to me. Do you think your mother would like these, she asked me, and of course I said yes even though she absolutely would not. In the same way, when he recommended drinking soup from the bowl there was really nothing else for me to say than that I would of course give it a go sometime.

Sometime! Never say sometime, for the reason that, unfortunately, with each day that passes that I don't drink soup from the bowl I feel terribly remiss, as if I am spurning him in fact, which is, naturally, an awful way for me to go on feeling. He was pleased with the suggestion you see, I could tell. I could tell it had been coming together in his mind throughout our conversation. He'd solved the problem you see—and that's the way some people are. They are ceaselessly finding ways of getting to grips with the world, of surmounting certain antipathies so as to apply themselves to it that little bit more. It's quite admirable really, how they refuse to let anything come between them and the rest of it—Oh, the rest of it! Sort of there, sort of hovering there all the time. Different ideas come to me now and again—strategies I suppose that might inculcate a little more compatibility. I just don't know if I'll ever get the hang of it if you want to know—as a matter of fact I think I've left it a little too late to cultivate the necessary outlook.

And the outlook, it seems, is everything. It's very difficult for anything to mean anything without that because without an outlook there is, obviously, no point of view. I open out the ironing board for the first time ever and set it up right by the window even though it's more or less completely dark outside by now. I find his two shirts in the laundry basket and decide I'll iron the darker one first—why a decision such as this came about at all I don't know, since both shirts would surely be ironed, and yet, inexplicably, it must have seemed as if one ought to be done before the other because when I laid both shirts across the ironing board I stood looking at them for a while trying to figure out which one that was. And actually I think the right choice was made because it wasn't long after I got started on the darker shirt that I began to feel very happy indeed and if you must know I was soon wishing there were more shirts of his for me to iron. I stood at the window ironing his two shirts for tomorrow, the darker one first, and I knew damn well how easily I could be seen. I don't know what's out there—I never could quite work it out—and all that time I spent behind the green curtains in the dining room at home, not getting any closer to it. And why shouldn't I stand at the window like this? Why shouldn't I be seen? I'm not afraid. Not afraid of any monster. Let it stand in the moonlit lane and watch me. It's been watching me all along, all my life, coming and going—and I don't know what it sees as it stands there, I don't know that it is not in fact becoming a little afraid of me—and I have to be doubly careful I think, not to frighten it away, because between you and me I can't be at all sure where it is I'd be without it.

Old Ground

S HE CLOSED THE EARTH over the green papers,
packing it down with her fists, more of a kneading
action than a pummelling so that she became quite entranced. Entranced by the movement, by the impressions
her knuckles made, and by the way she felt when she pressed
down. Love can be surprising. She couldn't locate where
that idea had come from, it didn't originate from anywhere
inside her. But it pleased her, and she leaned right into her
fists and pushed hard against the ground. Love can be surprising, she said, enjoying an unforeseen lightheartedness.
And then, modifying the mantra slightly, she put her skin,
eyes and lips close to her curled and muddied fingers and
whispered into them: Love must be surprising.

She swung her boots by the laces and hit them off the
wall, loosening neat wedges of dirt. Her mother opened an

upstairs window with a gloved hand and called down to her, but she ignored her mother, loathed the boots and flickered soundlessly round to the back of the house, her mother's voice chiming like uncertain fragments touching one against another in the breeze.

A red apple sat up on the lawn. Her brother stood at a distance from it, clattering garden snails together in his left hand which he lobbed one by one with his right, underarm, into the sky, with the aim of hitting them off the apple on their spiralling descent. He threw a snail at his sister. She peered up at it twisting through the air, issued a mordant ow sound as it landed several feet away and dropped her eyes to fix on the well-trained apple. The stupid apple. Leave it, he said. She stayed still and continued to frown at the apple. The stupid stupid apple.

She only imagined swooping down upon the apple, snatching it up in a vexed hand and hurling it against the side of the house. She only imagined the sound of its pips rattling, and the awful flat sound it makes when it hits the wall and falls apart. She only imagined these things but conceded, nonetheless, that her imaginings had to become more cautious, more subtle, perhaps, now that the blank card had come.

After a short time there was a shift—the apple held her

in its fluent green gaze as all thoughts and awarenesses in her began to softly trickle out across the garden. The windowpane flinched beneath its white sash. And then, of course, it was time for them both to go indoors and wash their hands.

Morning stands on its high swing and waits, shunting the dirt back and forth beneath its nails with a bare piece of card.